Love Notes From a German Building Site

Adrian Duncan is an Irish writer and artist based in Ireland and Berlin. He trained and worked as a structural engineer for over a decade, received his chartership from the Institute of Engineers Ireland in 2008 and later returned to university to study fine art. He has written a collection of short stories titled *Chicken-Lane Manifesto.*

To my mother, Jean

Love Notes From a German Building Site

Adrian Duncan

HEAD
ZEUS

An Apollo Book

LILLIPUT

First published in 2019 by The Lilliput Press
First published in the UK in 2019 by Head of Zeus Ltd

9 7 5 3 1 2 4 6 8

A catalogue record for this book is available from
the British Library.

ISBN (HB): 9781789546248
ISBN (XTPB): 9781789546255
ISBN (E): 9781789546231

Typeset by Marsha Swan

'There's dew on the grass,' Anna Sergeyevna said after a pause. 'Yes, it's time to go back.'

Anton Chekhov, 'The Lady with the Little Dog'

Introduction

I kept a notebook over the course of the job. I used it to archive the German words I required for communicating with the engineers, tradespeople and labourers on site. Sometimes, when I was looking up a word I'd spot an unrelated word nearby, become distracted and get drawn off into another part of the dictionary, often getting lost and forgetting my original intention. I put these forays into a section of the notebook that I titled, 'Love notes'.

das Werkʒeug – the tool
das Spielʒeug – the toy
das Zeug – stuff
Zeuge/in – witness
ʒeugen – to father
ʒeugen – to testify
das Zeugnis – evidence
die Zeugnisfähigkeit – fertility
die Fruchtbarkeit – fertility
die Frucht – fruit

I developed an interest in these lists of words, sometimes cross-comparing where I started and where I ended up, sometimes admiring the pivot in the list where the words moved in strange directions. I then began visualizing these lists as a series of arcs with centre points located around the object or idea they encircled. These points generated new if somewhat rudimentary views onto things that up till then I thought I knew well – I began to see the world a little differently.

At the end of this book I've compiled an appendix of what I consider the pointedly useful words I found. If you ever find yourself working on a building site in a German-speaking country, I'd say these words would be of some help. A few weeks back, while looking over the list of nouns and verbs, I realized the order in which they appear also suggests a narrative.

I decided to describe what occurred on the building site by using this sequence of words as a guide for my memories. I thought the best approach was to focus on three short intervals that occurred during the beginning (November), middle (February) and at the end (May) of the contract. These periods of time seem to me to be important because they led to a shift in my values, and me pursuing a course of action I had hitherto not seen as viable. This account is organized in sections, from 1.0 to 3.7, and it forms the backbone of the book.

While I was writing this, other ideas and items of interest came to my mind:

i. further 'Love notes', similar in character to the one above, but which are expanded upon greatly;

ii. a series of missives on particular ideas in engineering that I see as relevant to the text as a whole;

iii. some observations on individuals who are, or who, during this time, became, important to me – they are, my girlfriend Evelyn, my old dog Pearl, a labourer on site called Ivan, and my mother.

I've tried to arrange these components in as clear and artful a way as possible. Occasionally they drift into the timescale of the narrative arc, but I have allowed this to occur only when I think it will offer another worthwhile view onto the topic or idea under review. This necessary indiscipline, I hope, will also create some unexpected convergences between the elements. However, I'd imagine if you find any of these convergences satisfying, then it will be more so down to your sensibility for such accidents than mine.

Prologue

Evelyn and I arrived in Berlin in late November. Our tram eased to a halt across from our apartment block on the north-eastern edge of the city, and we disembarked. It was dark at that stage.

Power lines sparked as the tram trundled away and rounded a corner in the distance. We lugged our bags through a courtyard while snow drifted down onto the shin-high land-scapes of slush edging the perimeter. My hands were cold.

I'd an early start the next morning on a building site in the middle of the city. It was the first day of a short contract, and would be my last job as an engineer.

Next morning Evelyn accompanied me into town. The U-Bahn, dotted with dozing passengers, rushed past the city's pastel-coloured facades. Evelyn gazed out placidly as the sunlight, which was low and distant, fell across her face in intermittent flickers and bursts. Strands of her dark hair had fallen in bright loops from under the cuff of her white bobble hat.

We found a quiet café near the site, where we had a coffee and shared a croissant; then we went our separate ways.

That evening I got home late, and fell asleep on the couch beside her as we sat up listening to music on YouTube.

Part 1

November

1.0 *Flower of noise*

The second morning on site was a Friday, and it was dark, cold. I stood at the rear entrance to the property we were refurbishing, a low-slung building on the far southern edge of Alexanderplatz, waiting for Shane, a junior engineer who was here with our boss, Gerald, to prepare the place for the influx of subcontractors. Shane was a tall overweight young man from the Midlands – affable if at times gauche, but I grew to admire him over the course of the job. I gazed at the chunks of modernist real estate across the way, their exteriors reflecting the light from the street, then Shane rounded the site hoarding with a set of keys in his hand and some drawings tucked under his arm, and bade me towards the entrance of the building.

The place was a degree or two colder than outside. Glinting drips of water plopped throughout. It was a space constructed with square concrete columns supporting concrete slabs, and it smelt damp and unused. Six lamps, in a crooked receding pattern, drew the eye back into a sweeping brown darkness. The cables between the lamps traced drooping curves into the space, like diagrams of how the structure worked. We walked to the nearest lamp and Shane opened out his drawing so I could orient myself. The lift shafts, usually a good touchstone, had not yet been built. When I asked, Shane led me to the side of the floor where a rectangular section of slab had been removed. A series of steel props stood around the edges. I stepped between two and peered down at another rectangular opening below, then another, and it seemed this decreasing series of absences could have continued indefinitely were it not for the oily twinkle twenty metres farther down, in what would eventually become the lift pit. I looked up, through another propped void, then another, and beyond to the concrete ribs of the underside of the second-floor ceiling – the roof of this near-forgotten commercial property.

'Game consoles will be on this floor,' said Shane, 'games, computers, cameras,' thrusting a dirty finger at the plans. 'TVs on the top floor and above this kitchen appliances and the like,' and he peered around, 'hard to imagine.'

Each floor was enclosed with block walls, but ones that did not correspond with the level above. When we ascended a stairwell, from the rear corner of the ground floor up to the first, we were deposited at a ninety-degree angle to where we had entered below, and instead of being in the corner of a floor we were in the middle of a much larger one surrounded by an expanse of shadowy columns that seemed to belong to a totally different part of the building.

An hour later, by the time we'd made our way down to
the second basement, the bottom floor, I was utterly lost –
as if my short-term memory was being cleared each time I
emerged from the frigid staircases.

Shane was plodding quietly alongside me.

'I'm confused,' I said.

'Gotta take a leak,' he replied, and veered off, unbut-
toning his pants as he went. He turned behind a column a
few bays away and I could hear his piss spatter against the
concrete.

I slumped at the base of the column nearby, pulled my
old Nokia phone out and shone the wan display at the four
columns immediately to the north, south, east and west of
me – a cruciform of concrete poured in communist times.
The cruciform pattern was multiplied throughout this floor,
and duplicated on the floors above.

Shane reappeared, and as we continued on, a vertical line
of light materialized, edging a great volume of near-darkness
from which came small mechanical clicks and human grunts.
We walked down a corridor and rounded the corner to find a
wiry middle-aged man, who looked to be eastern European,
hunkered down and pouring petrol into a mechanical cutter. It
resembled a wheelbarrow but had a serrated blade as a wheel.
A fluorescent tube beamed on the ground nearby, casting
garbled shadows on the wall behind. The rest of the place
was black except for a lamp dangling somewhere at the far
end of the floor. The man looked at us, then went to the other
side of the machine, and started it. It rumbled and built to a

steady roar. Waves of burnt petrol wafted towards us. I knew the sound these machines made when the blade met concrete – an emphatic whine that seemed to resonate with the natural frequency of at least one my organs, and this sound, apart from rattling my eardrums, always made me feel ill.

I turned to Shane, stuffing my fingers into my ears and shouted, 'I've seen enough, let's go back to the cabin.'

The whine reverberated through the site, growing and receding as we climbed out of the building. It echoed in the stairwells, pealed across the floors, and when we passed the opening in the slab we'd peered into not an hour before, the yowl bloomed like a flower of noise, until we reached the exit, by which time it was relenting – and I was glad when we got back to our bright engineers' office, where I sat, removed my helmet and rubbed my head.

Our offices comprised six yellow cabins in three stacks of two at the top of a long, broad concrete ramp leading down to the west side of the lower ground floor of the building. Gerald's cabin was next door to ours. I'd seen him briefly the day before, pulling a roller suitcase behind him. He was tall, blond-haired and from Donegal. He, along with a number of others, had been taken on by this large British construction company who were snapping up out-of-work and desperate Irish engineers, managers and tradespeople to work on short-term contracts in far-flung cities in mainland Europe.

Shane, sitting at the end of the cabin eating a banana, peered at his phone then chucked it onto the table and said that Gerald wanted to see me.

'The fucker's in bad form,' he said, 'something's gone wrong in Leipzig; it's another one of these, just bigger.'

Gerald looked up as I entered his cabin. His hair, parted neatly, was swept across the top of his forehead, and he wore a pressed sky-blue shirt. He looked at me for a moment, as if he wanted to kill me, then he stood, smiled, put out his hand and said, 'Paul, good man, thanks for coming in. Get a seat there, I want a quick chat.'

We exchanged no further pleasantries, instead he quizzed me about my lack of site experience and frowned as I spoke, his green unblinking eyes judging my utterances and gestures. As I described the portfolio of buildings I'd designed over the previous fifteen years or so, I thought this was not a person with whom to try to gain an upper hand. He was a clever man who worked hard and expected others to take the world as seriously as he did, and, if you didn't think from the present and directly into the future of a project, you were usually wasting his time. He told me about our German-Irish clients – an electronics and appliances retailer – outlining to me not only the scale of this refurbishment but also their plans for expansion through eastern Europe. He explained the hours on site would be long, but that if I did well there'd be more employment on the horizon.

'And how's it looking out there now?' he asked, pulling his iPad from its sheath.

'It's a nice big job,' I replied.

'Are the lights up?'

'Just three left.'

'Get those up today,' he said, 'it all kicks off here on Monday and we have to be ready for the subbies.'

His accent was an ironed-out Donegal one that was probably once quite strong, but he must have realized that to become successful at management level he'd have to shift it east a couple of hundred miles towards Dublin, or at least towards the Midlands where it could flatten into the bogs. He was a middle manager at this time, but if he wished to climb further up the line then he'd have to decide whether to bring his accent further east to England, or develop it well out west, somewhere in the mid-Atlantic, where the floating voices of New England fishermen – fathers of a future management class of Boston, New York and Philadelphia – could inflect it. Then Gerald could begin to naturally corral phrases like 'I guess', 'for sure' and 'going forward' into his management-speak.

'Grand,' I said.

He looked at me. 'I want you to get a hang on the structural stuff out there – the lift shaft; it's a fucking mess, bring that together for me, okay? And have you much in the way of German?'

'I did a bit in school.'

'You better start remembering it,' he laughed, 'the company fabricating the structures are local, so prepare ... and before you go, I've a phone for you,' he said, handing me a smartphone, 'and when I call you on that, you better fucking take it. 'Cos I'm calling you for a reason, okay?'

'Fine,' I said.

He looked back at his iPad and I assumed he was finished, so I got up to leave.

'Good man,' he said, 'and don't bother come in tomorrow or Sunday, but rest the body for Monday. We go then, and we don't stop till we stop.'

'Very good,' I replied, as I stepped down from his cabin.

Love note 1

In my pocket dictionary, which I carried almost everywhere on site, these words come one after the other:

der Spann – the instep of your foot
die Spanne – the span (time)
spannen – to stretch
die Spannung – the tension, the potential, the voltage

Gravity, as it was taught to me in university, is understood as an invisible line connecting two bodies. It was once believed that outside of that line was void, until it became clear that there were many other tiny forces at play, and these tiny forces made up a continuous field of flux that all bodies are immersed in. The void then became a medium of electromagnetic forces.

When I first learned this, the universe became less lonely. Then, the more I thought about it, I realized that if I ever found myself in surroundings not to my liking the charges and forces that held me in place would prove impossible to overturn, or push away from me, or to change, and I would be left suffocating in an ever-strengthening electric field of unease unless something obliterated it and I was freed to begin again and meet the orbit of other things.

These thoughts started me awake one night two months before Evelyn and I left Ireland for Berlin. We'd struggled along for years in Dublin with part-time work, up to a breaking point about five months before we emigrated, when the rent of our apartment that we could barely afford anyway was put up. We left the shoddy part of the city we'd happily lived in for almost six years. I moved home to my parents in the south Midlands and Evelyn was with hers in north Leitrim.

In those four months apart I realized that I was more in love with her than she was with me. That night I woke perspiring into my bedclothes, I was anxious that if Evelyn and I stayed apart much longer then something would change irrevocably between us. So, the next day, I began searching for work outside of Ireland. Then I found this job in Berlin, and took it out of a quiet desperation to bring Evelyn and I back together – into the same city again, the same apartment – and perhaps align ourselves in a way that was similar to what we had before.

1.1 *Gridlines*

By two o'clock I was ravenous, so I left site and walked straight to the first Bratwurst vendor I encountered on the edge of Alexanderplatz, which was brimming with Christmas market stalls opening up for business. The vendor, dressed in red, was jigging over and back on a ragged square of cardboard laid out like a rug under his feet. I ordered two Bratwursts, ate the first savagely beside him, then the second as I walked along the side of the square. My hands were filthy, cold, sticky and drying up – the skin on the knuckle of my right index finger was broken and bleeding. I continued on under a bridge to a Dunkin' Donuts where I ordered a coffee and texted Evelyn on my new phone saying we should go somewhere this weekend, as it might be the last free one for a while.

I left the café and walked through the snow, back under the bridge that rattled as a train passed overhead. I re-crossed Alexanderplatz, which was now busier with people milling about the fragrant and twinkling market stalls, and returned to the cabin where I found Shane sitting on the ground, his legs splayed out before him – he was rewiring the plug for a heater. I realized he was the sort who liked being busy: as long as he was occupied he would be more or less happy, and if it meant sitting unselfconsciously on the bare floor of a cabin in the middle of Berlin and fiddling with a heater, then so be it.

'Done,' he said, plugging the heater in. It clinked distantly into life.

'Chilly out there,' I said.

'We'll be hugging that in a week. Gerald was saying the temperatures are to plummet. C'mon, we'll put up these lamps inside.'

The whine from the concrete cutter surged and receded through the building as we descended the gloopily lit stairwell to the lower ground floor. Four lamps cut swathes of light into the black expanse, ending as white lines on the edges of columns – the place had lost its volume and appeared as chalk drawings on folded pieces of black card.

As we worked, Shane told me that his father was a mechanic with a small garage on the edge of an uncle's farm in Westmeath. He told me about the Wall of Death his uncle and father built farther north into the bog, back the year he was born – a vertical tube made with scrap timber. 'Like something from a fairground,' he said. Apparently they slung themselves in clatters around this wall, for months on end, until a news crew came to do a feature and the place became swamped with visitors and they had to close it down before it fell apart. I described to him my mother and father and their bungalow near a single-street town on the southern edge of the Bog of Allen. I told him about my sisters and brother, then about Evelyn; and perhaps because Shane was still young, he responded bawdily to my mention of her, as if this is how men speak about women in the dark, suspended between two expanses of concrete. I tried to talk about football, but he said he had no interest.

There was something disarmingly innocent about him. Earlier, when a drill bit got stuck in one of the columns on the ground floor and he was up on the ladder banging at it with a claw hammer, he told me about a new type of sprayable concrete he'd been reading about, developed during the construction of a reservoir in southern France. As he hammered away at this drill bit, almost smiling at the stubbornness of it all, he began giggling at what they called this concrete. '*Spritz Beton*,' he said, a mock German enthusiasm jumping into his flat Midlands drawl. He cocked his head at me. 'Like it's a cocktail or something,' and he laughed again. Then, having returned to beating at the drill bit for a while, he stopped and with the hammer mid-air beside him, looked down to me. 'You know, I've an awful thirst for knowledge,' he said. I searched his pale face and narrow dark eyes for the smallest flicker of irony but he just returned to beating away at the drill bit, sending small dings out into the space.

When we finished hanging the lamps, Shane hooked them up to a distribution box near the middle of the floor and the place brightened a degree or two.

'We'll do the gridlines now,' he said.

I was hungry; the steel-toecap boots I'd been given were heavy and turning my joints to jelly. Shane wiped his brow, leaving a smear on his forehead like an Ash Wednesday blessing. He produced a ball of brickies' string and a can of spray paint from his jacket pockets and we worked in silence for the next five hours, pulling the nylon string taut against the surface of the slab, a metre to the right of a row of columns running down the length of the building, with Shane hunched over spraying a dotted line along it, sending spurts of yellow paint and dust up as he went. Then he straightened and plodded back down, writing GRIDLINE 4 at intervals along it. We marked out another, perpendicular to the first, running the width of the floor. The task was as arduous as it was precise, and when we came to the last ten-metre run I felt as if my body had emptied of glucose. I stood for a moment in the half dark watching Shane roll the ball of string up and it occurred to me that us drawing out these yellow lines was something more than representing a line on the architect's drawing as a larger, more-actual line on the structure's surface, it was something other than leaving the traces of someone else's ideas on the ground. I felt we were enacting an abstraction, but my thoughts crumbled around where exactly the abstraction occurred, so I decided that these intersecting gridlines one metre to the right of two perpendicular rows of columns receding into the distance were nothing more than beautiful because they forced me to imagine what this space might have looked and felt like before any of us got here, when it was completely dark. I wondered would the fatigue I felt in putting this tiny amount of light and order into the place be equivalent to what I would have felt if there was no light or lines and I was left to grapple the dark from what was incapable of being lit, by touching columns and the floor with my hands and feet, trying to demark what was substance from what was not, perhaps discerning what held the dark and what allowed the dark to remain in place.

It was past nine by the time we left and the traffic outside was all but gone. Shane walked off, running his knuckle along the face of the hoarding.

'See you Monday,' he said.

1.2 *A large-boned person in her late forties*

Next morning Evelyn and I took a dawn train north towards Rostock. The sun inched over the horizon as we left the north Berlin suburbs. We traversed a broad valley on an enormous red bridge whose three mountainous steel trusses rose and dipped like waves of orchestral music as we went. As the lines within lines of the structure shuddered and slid past I took a hold of Evelyn's hand and pressed it tight. She'd fallen asleep, her head resting on my shoulder. I pictured the bridge from down the valley, in side view, this proposition rippling across the land. The sun glared photographically through the girders, as if the patterns of structure had momentarily become shutters, so I shielded my eyes and looked to a patch of land below, where a ruined castle stood.

We zoomed past floodlands, through a tunnel, past gatherings of rooftops, under footbridges and road bridges, power lines, past frozen docks, around wood-edged plains with still deer watching from iced-over tractor-wheel ruts, then along endless hectares of exhausted minelands.

Hours later, as the train turned east towards the cliff town of Rügen, Evelyn woke and we looked out at the low midday sun scudding across the Baltic Sea onto the drenched beaches below.

That evening we took a walk on an empty strand that led to a range of cliffs. It was windy and we both wrapped up tight. I told Evelyn the place reminded me of a geotechnics course I once took in university, when we made a field trip to some cliffs south of Aberdeen, and how the professor of geology and us twenty young engineers walked through a cold mist circulating at the foot of those cliffs and examined the patterned swathes of compressed sandstone, granite and basalt drawing themselves out onto the faces of the land. The geologist, an excitable man in his late fifties whose name I couldn't remember, stomped around the beach outcrops expounding, through the breeze, on these enormous formations, which he claimed were mere glacially paced clouds trapped forever in dark sub-surface skies.

I turned to Evelyn, as we made our way along the underside of the cliff, and said, 'He was the sort that'd talk about geotechnics as if they were ghost stories about the earth and moon.'

'He sounds amazing,' she replied, pushing strands of hair from her face.

The sea thrashed behind her, then broke and came to shore.

That evening, after an almost painfully cold walk back, Evelyn and I took to our bed in a cosy guesthouse in the middle of town. She'd stripped to her underwear and when I got in she held my cold head onto her chest and I breathed. We dozed, then showered and went out to find somewhere to eat.

We ended up in a restaurant in the basement of an old granite townhouse. There was a football match on the widescreen TV above the bar and a group of young men sat underneath, racing to get drunk. They fell silent when we entered and eyed Evelyn as she passed. We sat across from each other in a timber snug. Evelyn had dressed far more formally than the venue might have asked, but it didn't bother her. Things like this don't bother her. She had put her dark hair up into a loose bun. Her eyes were bright, and her cheeks were still ruddy from the sea wind. The tables smelt of detergent, and the carpet of ancient beer slops.

A lady, a large-boned person in her late forties, came to the table and asked us what we'd like.

'*Nur zwei Biere, bitte,*' replied Evelyn.

Evelyn's parents are German and moved to Ireland in the late sixties. They speak German at home and as such Evelyn can speak the language fluently. When we first arrived in Berlin I envied this, but after a while I came to value the gradual growth of the language in me; I realized that to learn a language slowly allows you to savour its simple elements and the curiosities they stow. The lady smiled and left a slip of paper on the table beside us.

'A chit,' said Evelyn. 'They love paper. Everything is written down on paper.'

'*Alles klar!*' I said.

'Super,' she replied, '*du kannst gut Deutsch!*'

'I'm not sure how I'll cope on this site.'

'You'll be fine.'

'I won't,' I replied, 'I really won't.'

'*Der Balken,*' she said.

'What?'

'*Der Balken?*'

'What are you taking about?'

'It means a structural beam,' she replied.

'*Die Säule?*'

'No idea.'

'Column: *die Siegesäule,* the Victory Column. *Das Holz?*'

'Nothing.'

'Jesus, Paul, maybe you are fucked,' she laughed.

'What's *Holz?*'

'Timber.'

I put my face in my hands.

There was a noise from the bar: a penalty. The lady returned, and placed our beers onto the table. She blinked both her eyes and left.

'Seriously, you'll be fine,' said Evelyn. 'Bring a dictionary.'

'Gerald said as much too.'

'What's he like?'

'Grand.'

The young men were shouting at the TV.

'You're happy to be back working, though,' said Evelyn carefully. She was playing with a beer mat.

'I'm glad of the money,' I shrugged.

'I meant to say,' she said, 'I got an email from the museum in Cologne. They want me to do an art-handling course before I start. It's paid, but I'll be away for three weeks during February.'

'Art handling?'

'There's protocols before I can start.'

By the time we'd left Ireland Evelyn had secured a job as an assistant curator with a museum in Cologne, but the project she'd been hired for was postponed till the following August, so, when I got this job in Berlin, we decided to go ahead together then push on to Cologne after.

'You keen on that?' I asked.

'Can't wait,' she replied. 'It'll be something new.'

I looked at my beer.

'It must be nice looking forward to work,' I said.

'It is,' and she took a sip from her drink, 'but you know I know how you feel.'

A note on site-engineers' cabins

A building-site cabin is usually little more than a shipping container with a window and a door cut into it. Electrics are passed through the walls. The walls are then insulated and fitted with electrical sockets dotted high and low. A fluorescent lamp usually hangs from the ceiling. The cabin can accommodate up to eight people at a squeeze.

In a site-engineers' cabin, the door is usually left open. It's a strange space that links the abstract coding and decoding that goes on when designing a building with the noise and dust and problems emerging from the site as the building is constructed. You get little in the way of privacy there. The more important you are the less people you have to share your cabin with. It is possible to judge the nature of a construction company by how they arrange their cabins. If the site engineers share a cabin with the foreperson, or if the contracts manager shares with an engineer, or if the quantity surveyor shares with an engineer, then the company was probably set up by builders. However, if the contracts manager has a cabin to themselves, or if the contracts manager only shares with a quantity surveyor, then the company is run by accountants.

The cabins themselves can be easily stacked, one upon the other: raised gangways and stairways, all made from scaffolding and planks, are assembled to connect these rooms. Then, when the job is finished, everything is dismantled, the cabins are emptied, unhooked from the site's generator and lifted onto lorries.

In the winter they are grim places and a gallows humour often takes hold. In summer they are still grim, but when the sun is out they become more convivial and feel, with the theatrical shift in mood that accompanies the sun, like playhouses.

One day, when it had been raining and the floor of our cabin was traversed with muddied power cables, I looked around at the landscape of objects strewn across the place and decided to note what I saw.

> empty and discarded water bottles (various sizes)
> disposable coffee cups
> scrunched-up sheets of white cloth
> stacks of A3 and A4 paper in thin orange plastic wrapping
> a butter knife
> some brown cylindrical fuses
> cardboard folders
> pebbles

notepads

staplers

staples

tapes

sticks

spirit levels

chalk

chalk dust

chalk lines

a ball of string

spray-paint cans

pens

highlighters

a pair of scissors

laptops

teaspoons

tracing paper

lighting samples for the main retail floor areas

LED lights (both out loose and in packets)

coffee stains

cable ties

ink cartridges

ripped open ink-cartridge boxes

boots

jackets

vests

a used teabag (hardened)

screw-bits

masonry nails

plasterboard fixings

samples of guttering
bulbs
drills
a consaw
white sandwich-wrapping paper
a small toppled tower of silver washers
orange peel
a mound of instant coffee
cardboard boxes
dust
red ratchet straps
acetate
a small maroon book of heavy-duty fixings propped up on
    its side
a banana
a banana skin
levelling lasers
a tripod
a perfectly white serviette
a measuring staff
paperclips
hosing
signage
drawings
lustrous strands of copper
corrugated plastic sheets
bulldog clips
tubular chairs
a spare collapsible table
a glossy orange-and-black catalogue for plant-hire products

shiny black duct tape

red-and-white barrier tape

drawing pins

light-green pencils

plastic prism-shaped scale rulers

navy and black diaries

brown leather shoes

markers

scuffed white trainers

phones

orange towelling

phone chargers

a fluorescent light

white plastic wall panels

wires

insulation

glass

painted corrugated steel

flecks of rust

tramlines

sky

Part 2

February

2.0 *A yellow square*

I was sitting in our cabin on the last Thursday of February considering the location for a hole we needed to bore in a distant corner of the building when Franz, the owner of the company charged with assembling the larger parts of the structure, came to the door.

'Paul!' he said, grinning toothsomely. '*Du bist noch hier!*'

Franz could move easily between speaking English and German and he always spoke to me in German to encourage me, but I always replied in English to feel like I was helping him out too.

'Franz! Please come in.'

I opened out my drawing, indicating the position of the hole we needed, to which Franz responded with his usual elongated 'Mmm' and strode back out into the cold, pulling his phone from his pocket.

Moments later he reappeared, announcing, '*Mein Mann, Herr Dupke, er wird hier am Morgen um Sieben Uhr sein.*'

'Seven, tomorrow, good,' I replied, smiling, and left the cabin to mark out the hole.

The container filled behind me with the other engineers packing up to leave for the night. Franz took a seat to chat with Shane, who was sniffling with a heavy cold he was unable to shift.

The lower ground floor of our building seethed with workers and through the plumes of dust the whole place throbbed in a white light. I walked through the clangs, and the smell of burning steel and wet concrete, to the wall at the end of the floor and carefully sprayed out the yellow square.

On my way back out it began snowing again. I gazed up at the snow – coordinates tumbling through the black. My right leg shot out in front of me and I crumpled back with a crunch. I lay on the ramp, the whiteness swooning down around the silver buildings, all of them disappearing back up into the dark. My breath bloomed and dissipated. I blinked, and everything vanished.

I opened my eyes again to the buildings and the snow and the terrible pain in my knee. I was unsure how long I'd been out. Struggling up, I wrenched my limb out from under me. 'Mother!' I gasped, trying to stamp the pain off, but it was far too sore. I gulped and searched around, blinking. 'Mother.' White stars popped in my eyes and I thought I might pass out again. Grabbing my hard hat, I limped back to the cabin through the lamplit snow as my knee filled with a sickly liquid warmth.

Gerald was in our cabin looking over a drawing.

'Slipped on the ramp,' I winced as I sat down, grasping my knee.

'Is it bad?' he asked.

'Left knee.'

He looked at me, clicking his pen agitatedly.

'Go home and ice it,' he said, and turned back to the drawing.

I got to bed by midnight, but couldn't sleep and when my alarm sounded at six the next morning I was unable to move the joint. I worked it gingerly, then got back down to site as quickly as I could.

During the night someone had scrawled in huge red lettering BERLIN … BERLIN IS OVER down the length of our enclosure. The site security guard, a young man called Jochen, was surveying it. He shook his head ruefully. I stumbled along the hoarding and saw Herr Dupke parked up in a white van and sipping from a plastic cup.

I rapped on his window and he finished up his drink. He pointed to his watch as he got out, muttering something about me being late. He was lean, but barrel-chested, with a dark moustache, and wore a pair of spectacles with thick circular lenses that positioned his eyes a foot behind his head, and it was from there he appeared to look out at the world, always somehow catching up with it.

We made our way down onto the lower ground floor where, in my broken German, I pointed out the square and what we needed cored.

'*Na gut*,' he said, '*und wie lange gibst du mir, um dieses Loch ʒu bohren?*'

'*Wie bitte?*' I didn't understand his question.

'*Wie lange?*' he said, pointing at his watch.

'*So schnell wie möglich,*' I replied; it meant 'as fast as possible' and it was what I said to almost all of the Germans I dealt with. Its effect was beginning to wear off on them.

'*Gibt's hier Kabel?*' he said, pointing at the wall.

'*Wie bitte?*'

'*In der Wand, was für Kabel laufen hier?*' he said.

'What for cables?' I replied, peering at him.

This is how I received most utterances on site then, straining and spanning between whatever words I could gather in the moment. Most of what I missed was usually the kernel of what they meant.

'*Alles klar,*' I said.

He frowned, began to repeat himself, then shrugged and walked off.

On the way out of the building I came upon Ivan, a Bulgarian general operative – GO – who'd started with us a few weeks before. GOs, often also called labourers, are like the oil of the site, picking up all of the menial tasks between trades, tasks like emptying bins, carrying scrap to skips, or heavier work like breaking down and carting building materials to and fro. Ivan was standing alone at the bottom of the ramp. An open sack of salt slumped against the wall nearby and he was smoking a slim cigar, issuing great clouds of smoke and vapour that gathered around his head before drifting off. I asked him how his work was going.

'Good, en you?'

He gestured to my knee.

'Slipped,' I said, 'over there, last night.'

He inspected the patch of ramp. He was in his late forties, with black wiry hair and, though quite hunched over, he was still about the same height as me, which is to say he was of average height, but thin – in the way that labourers who smoke heavily are, all sinew and ash.

'Where in Bulgaria are you from?' I asked.

'Sofia,' he said.

He drew on his cigar. I asked if he'd any family, but before he could reply he glanced over my shoulder, ripped the cigar from his mouth, threw it to the ground and returned to where I'd fallen the day before, casting down salt dramatically, saying, 'No problem, no problem.'

Gerald was stomping down the ramp with his phone to his ear.

As he passed he put his hand over the mouthpiece and hissed, 'Massive fuck-up on site, boyo. Your corer has outed the whole fucking floor.'

'Bollocks,' I said, and hobbled back onto site.

2.1 *A pallet of copper offcuts*

Within an hour we'd restored power and the whole place quaked again. Two junior electricians snaked the cable away from the wall and Herr Dupke got back in behind his drill. Gerald took a phone call, cursed, and sprinted back to the cabins.

On the way back through the site I came upon eight metre-long metal tubes lying perfectly parallel to each other on the ground. I looked around, realizing it was one of Shane's most recent arrangements.

Earlier in the month, Shane had caught me in a quiet corner of the site making a tower out of pale blocks that'd been lying unused around the place. At the base of the tower I'd criss-crossed two fluorescent lamps. I was walking backwards to admire the construction when I heard him step from the shadows, giggling. I span round.

'How long have you been there?' I said.

He laughed, 'Oh about half an hour! What are you up to?'

'Dunno. I was bored. It's just messing.'

He eyed the thing glowing in front of us. '

'Don't say a word, will you?'

'I'll say nothing,' he replied, and ambled off.

A few mornings later, beside my computer, I found a tall mysterious stack of washers sitting in the middle of a square of mirror. I smiled; I knew he'd put it there. So in response, that afternoon, I leant six sweeping brushes in a line down a wall whose plasterboarding Shane was overseeing. And later the next day I walked past eight scaffold planks leaning against a wall on the lower ground floor, each plank six inches farther from the wall than the previous, making a strange octave of inclinations. The next morning I arranged a set of laser levels to project a perfect red square into the corner of a room he was working in.

We never acknowledged what the other was doing. It was a wordless language game we were building into the framework of the site. At first, what was essential to it was its near imperceptibility.

By this stage, however, certain tradesmen were beginning to notice these hindrances in their work areas, but nothing had been mentioned at management level so far, so Shane and I just kept doing it. Though I was happy to stay within the fabric of the arrangements of tools and materials on site, testing its limits, Shane, I realized as the days went by, wanted to move beyond it; almost as if he wanted his work to be seen.

As I stumbled up the ramp outside, I noticed it was bitterly cold, like the day had suddenly become a hysterical version of its earlier self. As I crested the ridge I saw Shane and one of the senior electricians smoking in the forecourt of our small shanty town of cabins. Our office brimmed with heads, shoulders and raised voices. I heard Gerald barking an order and the place went comically quiet. Someone else spoke and the cabin broke out in shouts; Gerald yelled again, and the place fell silent once more. Shane, snickering, told me that one of the ducters had caught Franz's lads pilfering a pallet of copper offcuts from the electricians and that they'd all been hauled in here to sort it out.

I stepped up to the entrance and caught sight of Franz at the far end, with Gerald standing between him and Dara, the foreman for the electricians – a rotund man from the south-west of Ireland who looked like he wanted to thump Franz's lights out.

It began to sleet again, so I pulled my bag from the cabin and made off for the canteen in the nearby Rathaus for something warm to eat. I went there most breaktimes with my book, Hans Fallada's *Alone in Berlin*. I'd bought it on a Sunday afternoon earlier in the month out of an English-language bookshop in Prenzlauerberg. Evelyn had just left for her art-handling course in Cologne, so I took a wander through the quiet streets of that part of town. The bookshop had seats at the back, and towards the front were comfortable old chairs into which people slumped, sipped coffee and turned the pages of their books. It was busy with American students conversing about what they were reading; to the point that one couldn't do any reading in the shop itself. I was tired and jittery and could feel the usual Sunday-night fear closing in on me. I had picked up a ragged second-hand copy of *Moby-Dick* from a basket in the rear of the shop when I saw next to it *Alone in Berlin*. I thought it a pretty maudlin purchase even at the time, but I didn't care. I chatted with an attractive young woman at the till who had short greasy blonde hair, as if she hadn't yet washed, and I imagined her running from her apartment that morning to catch a tram or bus. I asked her how long she'd been in Berlin, and she said a few years. I told her I'd just arrived. We both agreed that it was a lonely sort of place. 'Too lonely even for ghosts,' she said. 'Particularly in the winter,' I added, even though we both knew I had no frame of reference. She enquired if I was a writer too. I told her I was an engineer but that I often thought I'd like to write something sometime but certainly not now as I was so busy with this job, which I described to her, and she replied, in an edgeless east-coast American accent, 'That sounds really interesting.' She then mentioned her boyfriend had just finished another book by Fallada called *Short Treatise on the Joys of Morphinism*, which he had found insanely inspirational. I asked her if there was a copy of it here too and she pointed to a stack of them on the counter in front of me and laughed. I picked one up. It was small, with '€4' written in pencil on the inside cover. I said I'd take it.

I left the bookstore, Shakespeare and Sons, and walked across the nearby square, which was enclosed by glowing cafés and ice-cream parlours. Above were rows of high-ceilinged apartments. I pictured beautiful healthy carefree families in these warm apartments, enjoying their Sunday evening together.

I pictured the brown-and-white bungalow that my mother and father had built, one they made into our home and brought our family up in, and I thought about the type of shelter they gave me when I was a child, and how whenever I returned home to visit them I always found the house cold. I remember rarely ever being cold when I was growing up there, except perhaps after the baths our mother gave us, every Saturday night, when my brother and I were very young and we'd chase down the hallway afterwards with our towels around us, like two small superheroes, to the open fire in the sitting room where our father would dry us down at the same time, using just one towel. Then my brother and I would sit in front of the fire with our towels back over our shoulders and we'd not move until our pyjamas were given to us. Running between the bath and the fire, I thought – the hallway, with my small wet body exposed to the air – that was the only cold part I remember. I recalled other parts of my home: the back garden, the bedrooms, the kitchen, the front door, places where my parents and older sisters and my brother had been kind to me and I thought, at this stage of my life, my mid-thirties, that home had become less and less concrete and more something that merely housed memories of moments, a grouping of coordinates of light held overhead in the garret of my mind and I thought that, when my parents die, this garret will be blown open and will reveal a new immeasurable sky to me and I will either be the type of person who will expand into it, or be utterly crushed by the enormity of this new roofless expanse. I also thought, looking up at those apartments, if I was a few years younger I'd not be thinking like this; instead, I'd draw great fortitude from being alone and I'd strike out into the city to see what I might find, but I seemed to have lost that species of resolve. I moved on from those bright, comfortable-looking apartments because my feet were becoming cold and found a bar where I flicked through the books I'd bought and learned that Hans Fallada's real name was Rudolf Ditzen.

This name reminded me of some other place or time, but I was too tired then to pursue it so I just sipped my glass of Sekt. The next day on site I was flicking through the back pages of *Alone in Berlin* and noticed 'Rudolf Ditzen' again, so I sat up and googled it, and in among the search results of 'Hans Fallada' and 'Berlin' I saw a link to a Google map for Rudolf-Ditzen-Weg in Pankow; a narrow street that pierced an ellipse-shaped road called the Mayakowskiring, which was about a fifteen-minute walk from my and Evelyn's apartment, and off this Mayakowskiring there was another street named after a person: Boris-Pasternak-Weg. I searched for his name and learned that he wrote *Dr Zhivago*, and I remembered the movie adaption Evelyn and I rented one Sunday evening, years back, when we had first moved in together, and the enormous exotic slowness of it, and, because of its beautiful swirling soundtrack, how we both dozed off on the couch. Halfway through we woke when the music from the soundtrack rose to a crescendo, at which point we had no idea what had led us to that moment in the narrative, and we slowly roused, turned off the TV and the lights in the apartment and went to bed where we cuddled and twitched and fell in increments to sleep. Then, reckoning this Mayakowskiring was also important, I googled that and spotted, near the bottom of the screen, a black-and-white photograph of two tower cranes either side of a substantial building frame with an absurd half-built ball suspended in the air behind it. I realized this was the view of the hotel beside our building site, with the TV tower in the background, and this photograph had been taken from the ramp that led down to the lower ground floor of our site. The photographer was called Joachim Spremburg, and he was the official photographer for the then-in-power SED party whose leader, a Walter Ulbricht, he often photographed, but only in colour, it appeared. After a search for Ulbricht I learned that he lived on Mayakowskiring and I thought: *Ah, that's the connection!* I downloaded the photo of the hotel and TV tower, printed it onto a sheet of acetate, walked down the ramp and tried to eye it in among the buildings as they stood before me then. They lined up exactly.

2.2 A distant white planet

On the way to the Rathaus, I spotted Herr Weske, the
council engineer, standing like a knight at the doorway of
the ducters' cabin. He turned, spotted me and called merrily
across the yard, 'Paul, a moment, we have a problem.'

Herr Weske was in his late thirties, slim, prematurely
balding and what was left of his hair had gone almost
completely grey. He wore expensive rimless glasses behind
which were a set of blue eyes that searched with an animal-
like nervousness around your face as he spoke. However,
when he was correct about some mistake he had perceived
in our work, he was polite and calm and would describe the
exact nature of the problem he had detected so slowly that
it seemed he took an almost erotic pleasure from the disclo-
sure. He rarely spoke German with us and I assumed this was
because he could not bear to witness us sullying the language.

I limped over to him and he ushered me in. There were
three ducters to the rear of the cabin leaning back in their
chairs and reading newspapers.

'We have a big problem, on the lower ground floor,' he said. 'The hole, that is being inserted, that you are cutting out, it cannot go there.'

'Okay,' I said, 'we'll move the hole.'

He chuckled, 'It is already too late. I stopped your corer until this is corrected. I am the engineer from the council, Paul, and I have to make sure that no harm is done to the building by you all.'

He took his shining white helmet off and placed it on the desk. I knew he was going to gut me in front of the ducters who were glancing over every now and then. Herr Weske produced from his bag a hand-drafted reinforcement drawing dating from when the building was first designed. So carefully and slowly did he unfold and de-crinkle this handsome drawing that he seemed to be saying, *This is the care we show to our buildings and you lot coming in here should have the decency to at least show the same.* He pointed towards the elevation of a three-storey wall, running the tip of his index finger down the page until he stopped at seven thin diagonal lines, and said with what seemed disproportionate moment, 'You have just cut through those bars.'

'All seven?' I asked.

'Yes.'

'Are they important?'

'Essential.'

I began to feel unwell. Another mistake I'd have to report to Gerald, and they were building up. Though none of these errors of mine were showstoppers, they were accumulating at a pace that was creating tension between Gerald and me. It was becoming clear that I could not see the building site with the clarity that he could and it meant he could not trust me; and if he could not trust me, then his judgment had failed him in appointing me.

I felt Herr Weske staring at the side of my face, but I would not return his gaze. A ducter shifted in his seat. I looked at the seven diagonal lines in the middle of the drawing; then I looked to Herr Weske's fingertip, its neat nail and its white cuticle at the base, like a distant sun setting on a distant white planet, a planet I would happily have gone to there and then, and said, 'I see.'

'Yes, this is a big problem,' said Herr Weske once more. Then he took his phone from his pocket.

'I must ring my superior, the city engineer, immediately.'

Within a minute Herr Weske was pacing up and down the cabin having launched into a monologue to the city engineer about the problem he had uncovered.

He spoke so emphatically and at such speed that I failed to grasp what he was saying. The odd word would float up, but it would immediately be washed over again in noise, so I found myself just sitting there and waiting. I looked to the drawing, then I peered out through the doorway and spied a bird arcing over our cabins, like a rag thrown through the air.

Each Sunday in January, Evelyn and I visited a small café in Neuköln called Rook. Its walls were decorated with delicate prints of different birds from around the world. The first time we went there was a set of binoculars on the bench by the window and a book called *A Field Guide to the Birds of Europe and Britain*, a translation from an earlier German edition. I opened it at the cuckoo section and looked through the various drawings of cuckoos and jarheads. On the left-hand page were two line drawings of a cuckoo, mid-flight, the first showing its wings spread open, the one to the right with its wings thrust down, pushing the air beneath itself. I wondered who decided which image should go first in this illustration of moments of movement, why up, then down? I put the book away and thought then about the order of words in German sentences and how the active verb – the descriptive verb – was so often held breathlessly to the end. I thought how it was a strange way to speak, to counter-inform the material of the sentence in this way. When people spoke to me in German I always imagined the nouns and adverbs and adjectives lying inert across the line of the sentence until the last word, this verb, sprung them into life. I decided there was an inherent patience in listening like this.

Before, back in Ireland, whenever Evelyn spoke to her parents in German on the phone her voice would become softer and quicker. And if she visited them, particularly for any extended periods, by the time she came back to our flat in Dublin, all her English verbs would migrate a word or two east along her utterances. When we tried to speak German together in Berlin, we'd collapse in laughter but for totally different reasons – I sounded idiotic to her, whereas she sounded like a different person to me, like she was inside a glass globe, and our halting conversations were funny at first, but then they became uncanny.

The owner of this café in Neuköln was called François. He smoked a lot, stepping outside each time he finished serving a customer. He'd fill and empty his lungs expansively as he looked up and down the street. After a few visits he began chatting to us. He played a mix of seventies folk music and nineties electronica and if we stayed long he'd drop us out two tiny slices of cake before we ordered another coffee. Evelyn and I sometimes spent hours there reading books or magazines, with Evelyn making notes in her many slim notebooks. She'd open three or four of these notebooks at once, transcribing English and German scribbles and sketches from one to another to another, her mind working in strange, overlapping and ever-widening subsets of reference. She made these notes so diligently that she rarely noticed me peering at her. Then she'd stop, gather up her work and bind the notebooks together with a thin strip of leather – once a necklace her father had given her some years before – and look to me and smile.

During one of our last visits there, probably the last Sunday of January, François learned I was an engineer. He insisted I visit the Hauptbahnhof train station in Mitte and come back and tell him what I thought. He said it was enormous. So the next day I skipped off work an hour early and took an S-Bahn to visit it. When I disembarked, the wind, which I guessed was coming from the north, whipped through the capacious front foyer. The main body of the station held stacks of trains at different heights and depths sliding metronomically into and away from the platforms and people travelling up and down in lifts and escalators or wandering or darting across the vast floor areas. I thought it a pragmatic but inhumane volume of space – the structure was difficult to get a sense of all at once; its design, its glazing and its large grey trusses, beams and columns were fragmented and seemed to have been purposefully put out of reach. It reminded me, through its complete difference, of the roof structure of Antwerp train station.

Evelyn and I once visited Antwerp with her parents a year or so after we'd begun going out. It was an odd weekend break travelling around Belgium with them all, but there were three marble sculptures by a Vervoort the Elder that Evelyn's father Harald was interested in seeing and all of this gave the weekend some momentum. When I stepped onto the lower platform in Antwerpen-Centraal I gazed up at the roof construction way above me. I could not believe it. It was like walking beneath a canopy of unearthly, large trees, mid-summer. The lightness was there but the primary structure consisted of huge, red finger-like girders arcing up at intervals from either side of the station, meeting at their tips. The rest of the building seemed to be there only to hold those curves in place. I expected the bases of these girders to be massive, profound, that they'd plunge into huge foundations beneath the station walls either side: but I was wrong – they merely thickened along the belly of their lengths, curved down to the vertical then tapered into rounded nodes resting on ornate cast-steel beds, half a metre square, installed at eight-metre intervals along the length of the building.

As I exited the flank of the station I stared at this detail and how it told me, with unusual precision, about the delicacy of what was being transmitted to the ground, but it also told me the vast volume of space being carved out by the inside of the station was an illusion that just happened to be made with actual building materials. The spirit of this structure lay within the belly of its curved girders; it was a stiffness of its own making – all that was being put back down into the earth by these girders was that which had been taken from it: an enormous near-weightless volume of air, the spans of the glass on the roof and the weight of the girder itself. As we walked along the footpath outside, past these beautiful baseplates, I spoke about how graceful and human this was and how the small cast-steel base we could touch and run our hands over told us something of what it is like to be up on that roof, being that roof, and that the language of this station was not only one of ill-gotten colonial money but of another kind of conviction – organized man and machine foresight and a dominion of an expanded and intertwined mathematical and material imagination. I don't think Evelyn had seen me speak so abstractly or so animatedly in front of her parents before, but out of courtesy they shared my enthusiasm, the enthusiasm of someone who has not seen very much. We then visited the Rubens House in the middle of Antwerp, a devout, umbrageous place, but all I could think about for the rest of the holiday was that railway station roof being constructed, and the sun shining on those girders as they extended upwards to the moments where their tips ineluctably met along the roofline.

A skip clanged to the ground outside. I looked to Herr Weske who was putting his phone away; he appeared displeased. I asked him what we needed to do about these repairs, to which he grabbed his drawing, folded it over and stomped out.

'Herr Weske,' I called after him, 'what's the problem? How should we proceed with your repairs?'

He turned and walked back to me, his head bowed, and whispered, '*Paul, bitte verzeihen Sie mir, ich habe über die falsche Zeichnung gesprochen.*'

'Ah,' I said, realizing he was apologizing for referring to an incorrect or superseded drawing, 'but do we have to do anything further?'

He just shook his head, turned and made his way down the ramp and back onto site. I stepped from the office and looked at our engineers' cabin across the way – it had calmed and was beginning to empty. I rounded the corner and shuffled off to the Rathaus on the eastern side of Alexanderplatz for my lunch.

As I walked, I looked back at the site and I could see my co-workers dispersing back down the ramp and across the courtyard of cabins. Most of them were laughing.

A note on the types of games
played at management level

Over the course of a project, a building site changes greatly in mood. It goes from being a very serious place to being a playground and back. Then, just before the job is finished the site becomes utterly serious again, up until it is 'brought across the line' and the building is handed over to the client and opened. When the building site is gone, then the memory of it, its archival version, is reconstructed elsewhere and another game is played, an entirely serious game involving the principals of companies arguing for payments, power and reputation.

At this point, our site was entering its first game stage. The place was so full of workers, tradesmen and labourers carrying out so many different tasks at once, that if you tried to make sense of the chaos you would probably waste a lot of time. Management had to wait for the chaos to begin making sense, or for some pattern of progress to emerge. While they waited for this pattern to form, like silt settling onto the bed of a huge rushing river, management would become a little impotent, even bored, and they would fill that brief period of time with games, all of which were one-upmanship games, sometimes quite brutal, but there was always a clear victor. I had noticed over the previous few weeks that Gerald was masterful at these games, and because the thoughts of appearing impotent or redundant to anyone was distasteful to him, he would infuse the spirit of these games into the dealings of the site. The games he played happened at management level. The labourers and tradespeople were not direct players – their part in the games that Gerald played had a detached vicariousness.

During a meeting in early January a series of complaints had been made directly to the client about the cleanliness of the site. The source of these complaints was a subcontractor, a small Englishman called Stuart, who was designing the sprinkler system. Gerald took some heat for this complaint at the time, but at a subsequent site meeting he calmly informed the project manager that everything would be sorted out by the following week. Gerald also registered his thanks then to Stuart for bringing this issue up so forthrightly with the client, and we moved on to the next item in the meeting schedule. Later that evening when the site was closing up Gerald came down to our office and bawled out Shane and me for many minutes. Then, by the end of January, when the site had become a game, Stuart, during a meeting, brought up that he needed to carry out some testing on his sprinkler system from the start to the end of February.

Gerald ensured that all four tests that Stuart required could only be carried out on four consecutive Saturday night / Sunday morning shifts between the hours of 8 pm and 8 am. When Gerald tabled this testing schedule at this meeting in late January everyone knew what was happening and there were smiles passed around the cabin. Gerald proposed this schedule in such a way as to suggest that there was no malice or pettiness to it, just that he wanted to be as rigorous and committed as Stuart had been in early January when he grumbled to the client about the cleanliness of the site. When the project manager accepted this proposal, Stuart sat there digesting that he would not be able to go home to see his wife and kids for the next month and that those four consecutive weekends were ruined, but he also knew that he could not complain, that he had to take it and do it like it was no problem at all, like water off a duck's back, and each Monday morning through February, during this period when Stuart was carrying out his testing, he would come into site late, looking tired, and Gerald would always ask him: 'Get up to much yesterday?'

'Nah, just slept,' Stuart would reply.

I often wondered if Stuart would try to get Gerald back, but if he did, it would have to be a killer blow or else Stuart would get it harder the next time. You need to have the stomach for this kind of game playing – some are good at crushing others, some play the game with brutality, but others play it with brutality and humour, and those were the ones who seemed to me to be admired.

Love note 2

das Blatt – a sheet of paper
das Blatt – a leaf

Not far from the building site was an old newspaper publishers, upon the roof of which a circular *Berliner Zeitung* sign rotated perpetually. One afternoon – I can't remember exactly when – but I was on the roof of our building with a labourer, who was pushing insulation into a hole that was leaking rainwater into the floor below, and I could not recall the word for pressure.

drücken – to push, to hug, to press
der Druck – pressure
der Druck – printing (reproduction)
drucken – to print
die Druckerei – the printing works

During the summer months in Berlin when the sun is out for weeks on end and you are cycling down the streets lined with linden trees you can feel, on perfectly clear days, the sap falling from the trees like light rain.

When I first felt this I imagined the sap being pushed out onto the leaves. I thought the whole tree was printing itself onto the surfaces of these leaves – that the trees, swaying and bobbing and perspiring and dripping in the breeze, were publishing themselves in many daily editions.

> *das Löschblatt* – blotting paper
> *löschen* – to extinguish
> *löslich* – soluble (as in water)
> *lösbar* – soluble (as in a problem)
> *die Lösung* – the solution

In those instances, while pedalling along, I'd think about the nature of problems, and some of the types of categories they might have:

1.0 Problems that can be solved
    1.1 Problems that can and should be solved
    1.2 Problems that can but should not be solved
2.0 Problems that can't be solved
    2.1 Problems that you don't want to solve
3.0 Problems that you want to solve
4.0 Problems that you need to solve
5.0 Problems that you understand
6.0 Problems that you don't understand
    6.1 Problems where your lack of understanding of the framing of the problem is inherent in the problem
7.0 Problems that emerge from solving other problems
    7.1 Problems that lead to stillness

7.2 Problems that lead to excess

8.0 Problems that are pleasurable to solve

9.0 Problems that are pleasurable left unsolved

10.0 Problems that you are aware of

This line of thought suggests to me that a person's nature is a function of their attraction to certain types of problems and if this attraction changes over the course of a person's life, and if one reflects on these changes over time, then the pattern of these changing problems offers a view onto their personality and how it might have evolved.

A note on how an engineer sleeps and wakes

When engineers wake at night, particularly when they are working on a large and stressful project, their dark and malformed thoughts often conflate with what is unknown in the molecular make-up of the material about which they are fretting.

2.3 *This is no way to treat a man*

The Rathaus, though very busy, had been muted; and so strange and distracting was the atmosphere that I read very little Fallada. When I returned to our cabin, Eugene, a clear-eyed senior engineer from the Ukraine who I became fond of over the course of the job, was sitting at his computer looking at YouTube clips of old Pathé newsreels. He usually disappeared on his own for lunch, wandering away from the cabin, gazing up at the snow and the buildings, as if he had never seen such things before. I got the feeling that he liked me and would happily have organized for us to lunch together. We went for coffee one afternoon, a day or two after he first arrived, and spoke about structural designs and buildings we'd worked on in Dublin during the boom, and how fast and corrupt everything was and how quickly it all disappeared. He was an intelligent man and was a calm part of the office.

'I see the temperatures are to drop from tomorrow afternoon,' he said without turning from his screen, 'down well below freezing. I hope this doesn't ruin our concrete pours … Gerald showed me the new timeline for the contract this morning – it's crazy, way too little time.'

'I know,' I said distractedly as I swung back in my chair, 'these pours …'

The cabin became quiet. Eugene put on a set of head-phones to listen more closely to the film clip playing on his screen.

My laptop pinged. An email had popped up from one of the tradesmen on site. There was a clash somewhere on the second floor between an air-conditioning duct and an outfall sewage pipe. I gladly forwarded the email to Shane, who was in charge of that floor.

This is how we spoke to each other about the work on site – almost all of our communication happened in emails, all traceable lines of group communication. We received information, digested it, discerned who best to send it on to and disseminated it as such. Then we'd leave the cabin and enter the dusty, noisy and chaotic building site to find where and how this command was being carried out and report on its progress to Gerald, and he collected all of the tasks and their status into a weekly progress report for the project manager who worked directly for the client. This project manager would then report every fortnight to the client's executives on how the site was generally progressing. Within that hierarchical flow the progress was then boiled down for the client's CEO to two questions, a) is the store on time? and b) is it on budget?, and if the answer to both was 'yes' then we were all doing well, and would be allowed to continue unhindered. The details of the progress itself was incidental other than perhaps as amusing anecdotes these executives might tell each other, second or third hand.

These meetings we had on site each week were where the more granular elements of the project were discussed. They went on for hours and, because I always had at least one structural issue to answer for, I had to sit through the whole thing, in one of our cramped containers, with two grey desks set out end to end, where eighteen other men sat around either answering questions, or eating biscuits, or looking on their phones as we systematically analysed every feature of the job, describing progress, defending delays or deflecting blame. It was during these meetings that I began to develop my disdain for the pointlessness of this kind of endeavour. By the middle of February, usually after I had finished describing to my colleagues any structural issues on site and the shopfitters began describing their progress, two questions would appear to me: Why am I sitting here? and, How has this happened? Each week I tried to pursue the answers to these questions, but my thoughts always stopped at the same answer, one that I did not believe: that I am this way inclined. After the shopfitters' report we'd progress to the flooring contractor, a man in his early fifties from Birmingham, who was as funny as he was succinct, and the atmosphere in the cabin would shift, and I would stop pursuing these thoughts. Then the project manager would go through the 'client concerns and consents' section, which in the minutes, for the entirety of the job, had the words 'no change' written beside it. Then just as everyone stood and put away their phones to return outside and get some fresh air, the project manager, Leonard, a slight, tenacious man in his early sixties with thinning white hair always asked, 'Any other business?' and each week the following set of minutes would state, beside this heading, a terse, artless 'none at moment'. Each of the specialist subcontractors – the electrical designers, the air and water engineers, the sprinkler-system designers – were British companies and all were represented each week by men in their late forties. This sort of work was so familiar to them that I often wondered how they summoned the will each morning to get out of bed, to repeatedly oversee the installation of these overdesigned systems of standardized materials. But if anything went wrong, these were the people to solve the problems, from first principles up, and that was their value, bringing deviations from standard back on track, and I wondered, each week when they rolled into Berlin, if they must have wished for a truly great problem to emerge from the chaos of the site to somehow challenge them. Then I'd hear them speak in the meetings, and every time they answered a query with an 'as per Poznań' or an 'as per Belfast' or a 'same detail as Bologna', it became clear to me that there are no new problems in buildings like this and that the fundamental challenge is in retaining flow, which is possible only if we try to increase the speed of installation so much that it might briefly sate the will of industry.

The sleet outside the cabin had begun swirling itself, every now and then, into snow. Eugene's chair creaked behind me as he stood to look out the window. The trams had slowed. Soon the snow was whirling down. Huddled right up into themselves, people dashed to and from the tram stop or dived for cover into the cheap clothing chain that had opened up across the way. Even the bobbing network of red-clad Bratwurst vendors had abandoned the square and formed a steaming line under the canopy of the sportswear store opposite. Commuters disappeared down the U-Bahn entrance and the whole junction went very still, as if it was awaiting something far larger than weather.

Shane stepped in; he looked tired. Snowflakes covered his head and shoulders. He sat heavily, sneezed three, four times, then got up again, closed the door over, sat back down and rubbed his nose with a disintegrating ball of tissue paper. He was in terrible form, run down, and had been unable to get rid of this cold for weeks. I suspected that his artistic interventions in the building site were beginning to be made late in the evening, long after everyone had gone and sometimes into the night.

A GO appeared at the door with snowflakes sliding down his hard hat: he asked if there were any fuses. Shane sneezed again, then handed him the keys to the cabin we used as a meeting room and said to take the fuse out of the toaster. The GO ran off and out of habit left the door open behind him. Shane got up and closed it. Brian, a junior site engineer, then blustered in and took his seat beside Shane who asked him to shut the door over. But Brian needed to send an email. He turned to us saying it was a fucking joke us relying in this way on the quantity surveyor's broadband signal. 'Fuckers are too mean to get us one,' said Shane, and we nodded. A few seconds later Andy, Gerald's assistant manager, came in from his lunch and stood at the door complaining about the cold in his near incomprehensible Kerry accent. He took his jacket off, shook the snow from it, then put it back on and took his seat by the window at the end of the cabin. Shane coughed coarsely, closed the door over again and tugged the electric heater towards him, then Brian pulled it back. Shane relented, got up and left, slamming the door. We looked at each other. A tram rumbled past, as the edges of the windowpane filled with dabs of snow. A shiver ran up my legs as a gritter scuttered by spraying salt onto the footpaths. Shane returned and slammed the door behind him once more. The walls of the cabin rattled. He sat down sullenly and Eugene, as if he was Shane's father, told him, 'Take it easy there, lad.' Another GO appeared at the door and asked Shane if he could borrow the keys for the store room, and as he was about to close the door the other GO reappeared returning the keys for the meeting room. He ran off, leaving the door swinging in the wind. Shane pulled it to again and sat shaking and sniffling; we looked to each other. Then Gerald, opening the door a crack, stuck his head in. Shane span around and I thought he might slam the door on Gerald's head. Gerald frowned at him, then turned to me and said, 'Did you get that email I sent?'

'Not yet,' I replied.

'Check it now,' he said, 'it's urgent,' and he disappeared.

I peered over at Shane. 'I need a bit of broadband there.'

He stormed out, leaving the door flapping. He made off around the corner of the storeroom container where we could hear him screaming at the top of his voice, a sort of tremolo of frustration howled wordlessly into the snow that must have been flurrying around him very beautifully. We chuckled. I refreshed my screen, and Gerald's email popped up. I went to the door and, through the torrents of snow, called Shane back. He came to the corner of the container, shivering, and shook his head. He was being pelted, so I ran over to him, put my arm around him and assured him, shouting through the squall, that we'd get this nonsense sorted out and I told him it was no way to treat a man. His small dark eyes were not so much angry as sad, and I promised I'd go directly into Gerald to make sure we got another broadband box for our cabin so we could work in comfort, and maybe, in the meantime, I suggested he might trade places with Brian for a while, at least until he got over this cold. His shoulders were fleshy under my arm and I thought he was going to cry, really sob, so I took my arm away and gave him a puck on the shoulder, saying, 'Come on in to fuck, before they think you've gone mad.' He shrugged, followed me in, and sat down. I closed the door over and stood at it for a while and Eugene, forcing a laugh, regaled us with a story about an old colleague of his, a Bavarian chap – a hard drinker, apparently – who'd got the sack from a site in Karlsruhe after a foreman grabbed a forty-foot aluminium ladder this Bavarian had been using at that time. When the foreman turned the ladder in his hands, a rumble developed along it, which grew louder and louder until, with the foreman utterly confused, hundreds of tiny bottles of *Kräuterlikör* slid out of the rungs and bounced and smashed at his feet. The Bavarian was chased off site. We laughed. Then, after riding out one of those strange collective silences often found in offices, we began marvelling at how much the German lads drank on site, after which we fell quiet and returned to carrying out our tasks.

I gazed out the window. The snow had eased off and the street movements had settled. I fingered my knee to find where the pain, which was oscillating between dullness and keenness, was most acute. My phone buzzed: it was Franz.

'Can you talk?'

'What's up?'

'This copper cable business,' he said.

'Have you got the pallet back?' I asked, stumbling out of the cabin.

'It's an hour outside of Berlin. My guy says he won't, with the snow, get it back into town. Can you get Gerald to halt the police? I promise by the morning I'll get it back.'

I called up to Gerald, he was sitting at his desk looking over the programme for the job. I told him Franz had been in touch.

'Is this not just more of his bullshit?' he said, still looking at the drawing.

'Probably,' I said.

'We don't have time for this nonsense. You know there's a royal visit tomorrow, right?' he said, as his phone beeped. He picked it up.

My heart fell. These 'royal visits' were days, one every six weeks, when the client's executives visited. They were arduous days given over to making the site look busy but in a controlled way, which meant suspending messy works like this coring I'd organized. This, I knew then, would cause a delay, which would be brought up at the next site meeting. Then the project manager would put a series of questions to me at the meeting that would eventually lead to me being asked, 'Why was this hole not bored earlier?' and I would then have to manufacture some unenvisionable circumstance that caused this mistake, and this unenvisionable circumstance was either believed and the delay it caused would then slip into the ether of the programme, or I would be scoffed at and the delay would be noted and would become an issue at the end of the job when the conversation about money and contracts would happen, but worse, I would be thought slightly less of by the rest of the management team.

Gerald put his phone down, looked to me, and said, 'Herr Weske called me earlier, apologizing for holding us up. I didn't know what he was on about.'

I shifted my weight. 'He came in all hot and heavy about some supposed error we'd made, but he was looking at the wrong drawing.'

'Ha!' said Gerald, smiling broadly. 'Nice the shoe being on the other foot for a change. Did you give the fucker a kick?'

'I didn't,' I replied.

'You know he'd close us down if he got the chance. You should drag him over the coals for this.'

'Fuck it,' I said, 'it's gone now.'

Gerald looked at me and in the brief silence I detected the difference between us: where he relished the games that course through a building site, I could barely see them, never mind understand their rules. And I think he read this apparent ambivalence as an insult to the way in which his profession encompassed him.

'And how's that corer getting on with that hole down there?' he asked.

I'd completely forgotten about Herr Dupke.

'That has to be done today,' said Gerald, looking right at me.

I left the office as calmly as I could, then lurched down the site ramp and into the lower floor. I rushed, through the din, to the rear wall, but Herr Dupke was gone and only three quarters of the hole was finished. There was no sign of his tools either. It was two minutes past three. *You lazy prick*, I thought; then he appeared around the wall and strolled over to a jumper he'd left on a stack of pallets.

'Herr Dupke!' I called, and asked him if he could finish the work. '*Können Sie das fertig machen?*' I said.

He shook his head, then grabbed his jumper and left. I hobbled after him shouting that we needed the hole done today.

ADRIAN DUNCAN

He turned and I think pretty much told me to fuck off.
So I informed him, in my terrible German, that if he did
not finish the hole today that we would not pay him. He
advanced on me and pushed his dusty hairy face up close.
His eyes glowed distantly and he said, '*Wenn du mich nicht
bezahlst, dann find' ich dich und werd' dir die Beine brechen,*'
which I took as a threat that if we did not pay him that he
would break my legs.

'*Du Scheisser, du Scheisser,*' he continued viciously,
prodding me in the chest and informing me that any delay
caused was by me being late that morning, '*du bist hier heute
zu spät da gewesen – ich nicht!*' he said. '*Ich musste auf dich
warten.*' Then he launched into what I perceived as a broad-
side on how we ran our site, which came to me as a stut-
tering amalgam of noises and words: '*Zu viel*' (too many)
– '*dummes Sicherheitszeug auf dieser Baustelle*' (stupid secu-
rities on this site) – '*Wie können wir*' (how can we) – '*unsere
Arbeit tun?*' (do our work?). '*Wie können wir so arbeiten?*'
(how can we work this way?) Then, cutting the air with his
hand he drew close again and snarled a few words that told
me he could see right through us and he could tell we knew
nothing about building: '*Ihr habt keine Ahnung, wie man baut.
Faul, dumm, idiotisch. Das seid ihr – dass ist alles.*' As he
made to pass me he asked me why were we all here. '*Wofür
seid ihr eigentlich alle hier? Du Scheisser,*' he said, pushing
past, '*bah! Die totale Scheisse.*'

He walked off. I pursued him, apologizing. I pleaded, but
he was having none of it. At the bottom of the ramp he turned,

me still calling after him – he probably felt sorry for me – and indicated that I finish the hole myself. '*Stemmen*,' he said, meaning that I use a concrete breaker. Then he stomped off. I watched him climbing the ramp until he disappeared.

I felt my phone vibrating in my pocket; it was a message from Evelyn. *Can't wait to see you tomorrow!* I smiled, put the phone back into my pocket and walked carefully back up to the cabins.

It was almost four and all the German labourers and tradesmen and GOs had left the site. I texted Franz. *I can help you with the police stuff, but I need you to give me a hand here this evening.*

Kool, he texted back, *but is the police thing definitely okay?*

Love note 3

die Zahl – the number
das Zahlwort – the numeral
ʒahlen – to pay
ʒählen – to count
erʒählen – to recount, to tell
Ich erʒähle Dir davon was passiert ist – I will tell you about
   what happened
davon – there from

Therefore:

Ich erʒähle Dir davon was passiert ist – I will tell you, there,
   from what happened

One day I stole away from site for a few hours to meet Evelyn at an exhibition of minimalist art at the Neue Nationalgalerie, way over west near the Potsdamer Platz U-Bahn station.

I passed the angular yellow Philharmonic buildings on the right and walked up to the dark, bunker-like Neue Nationalgalerie. The building, despite its size, crept up on me, its glass frame sitting up there on an enormous concrete pedestal.

To the rear was a sunken garden dotted with frozen statues and water features. I entered the building through a door propped open with a small timber wedge and continued across the floor – an empty vitrine. In the distance a man emerged from below. He gestured me towards him, so I walked to the stairway and descended to the galleries in the lower levels. Evelyn was there, turning from the reception desk with two tickets in her hand. She looked excited.

We entered a dark room in the middle of which was a 16 mm projector on a timber plinth. There were about twenty other people ghosting about. Someone flicked the projector on and the film began to whirr. Onto the wall the arc of a large circle was enscribed by the projecting light. Behind us other machines clicked into gear, releasing dry ice into the space that puffed across the emanating light, suddenly making the white inclined surface of this arc apparent. We approached this horizontal form completing itself in the dark. Everyone else drew closer too, as if we were druids around a sliver of winter solstice light.

I whispered to Evelyn, 'What's this called?'

'*Line Describing a Cone*,' she whispered back.

Someone walked through the projection, greatly disturbing the dry ice universe. Then Evelyn stood to one side of the cone and thrust her finger into the wall of light. It looked as though she was dragging the skin of the object back, revealing a nothingness within. I ventured towards the rear wall and stood beside the slowly completing circle for some time. The projector clattered along comfortingly. People stood in a line, surveying the length of the thing. I thought of the name of the piece, *Line Describing a Cone*.

I approached the projector, closed my left eye and aligned my right with the lens. The cone suddenly flattened into a tube, one with almost perfectly parallel walls. I considered the implications of this parallax, and the distance between the tiny circle inscribed on the film and the filament of the lamp in the projector. I gazed along the tube until it completed itself. The room plunged back into darkness and the 16 mm film thirstily uncoupled from its mechanism. I stood still, waiting for the house lights to come up. When they did, almost everyone had dispersed and I could see Evelyn looking over at me, blinking.

We kissed goodbye outside and I rushed back to site. As I sat in the train surging through the dark tunnels underneath the centre of Berlin, all I could think of was the small circle on the projector film pouring itself onto the larger one on the wall, like one 'o' echoing another. It was then I realized how drawn I was to the idea of the contours of language and words and letters as firmaments that lie across and through the actual world.

> *bohren* – to bore, to drill
> *bohrend* – piercing (adj.)

Bohren was the first German word I learned on site; it was while I was trying to instruct Franz's builders as to what was required to build the lift-shaft walls. The place was jarringly noisy that day as I stood in front of one of the older tradesmen, us two shouting hopefully at each other through the din. I scrambled through my dictionary trying to locate this verb, to describe how we'd bore our three reinforcement bars through the edge of the slab, to connect *verbinden* with the vertical reinforcement *mit dem senkrechten Eisenstück* that penetrated the first floor slab *die durch die Platte in dem ersten Geschoss einführen*. As I uttered these instructions I found myself miming movements of this kind: for 'connection' I'd push my fist into my hand; then, to show the three reinforcement bars I'd stick the three fingers of my left hand upwards and interlink them with three fingers from my right hand hovering overhead, to suggest their connection to the three horizontal bars in the floor slab above.

Sometimes in desperation we'd scribble a drawing of what we meant onto a nearby column and in a culmination of all of this we'd close in on what it was we meant. Whenever I alighted on the correct word this tradesman's eyes would open a little and he'd nod. He was a patient, clever, precise sort, and we agreed each time we talked over this lift shaft that it was a crazy way to go about building it. '*Verrückt!*' he would say, and I'd tell him that it was part of the previous agreement, the *Vertrag*, and we'd shake our heads and usually, before I walked off, he'd put his hand onto my shoulder and look directly at me and laugh somewhat manically, before letting me know that he understood. It wasn't just the language he understood, or the fact that we shared a comprehension of the poor planning that had gone into this part of the structure; it was as if he understood far more. '*Ich verstehe*,' he would say.

2.4 *A drink near Schlesisches Tor*

By eight o'clock the site was empty. I stood at the base of the ramp with a jackhammer at my side. I'd no idea how heavy these things were. By a quarter past eight there was no sign of Franz. I called him. He didn't answer.

'Fuck him,' I said.

I knew I wouldn't be able to hold the jackhammer aloft for long, so when I returned back to the hole I built a structure to support the tool, using three A-frame ladders – two standing at either end of another laid horizontally on top. I unfolded yet another behind, clambered on, and began breaking out the last part of the hole.

Within a minute the ladders were hopping back and the jackhammer was twisting out of my hands. They were the most pathetic hands in the city. I began to sweat, and the dust and bits of concrete were pinging back in my face and I could see how pointless it all was. I relented. The tip of the jackhammer slipped down the wall, the handles spun out of my hands and with that the ladder flipped and clipped my chin and the whole construction collapsed around me. I sprawled among the ladders, then scrambled over them to unplug the roaring jackhammer. I picked myself up and held my chin. It was pouring blood and a chip from a lower incisor floated around under my tongue. I spat it out and staggered across the floor, back out to the row of Portaloos at the side of the ramp to wash my face. My hands were covered in blood. The Portaloos were dark and filthy and were no place to wash any cut. I gathered up two balls of paper, put one to my chin and returned to the cabin, put on the lights, grabbed Eugene's sparkling water and poured it over my wound. The water was cold as it fizzed down my neck and chest. I ground my teeth, shook, and thumped the table. I growled. I looked into the window but couldn't see myself clearly, so I took a photo of the cut. It wasn't as bad as the amount of blood suggested. I sat and washed it out again, and brought the first-aid box up onto the table and fumbled around for a plaster. Jochen, the site security guard, came to the door.

'Paul,' he said, 'you are here!? Are you ok?'

I peered at him, replying, 'Ah, Jochen, yes, unfortunately, grand.'

'Can I see it?'

He looked, winced, then nodded. 'Yeah, it's not too deep, it's okay. Do you want me to put a plaster on?'

I could see over his shoulder that it was snowing again, but I held no more romance for snow. When Jochen finished dabbing my chin he placed a plaster across the cut and asked how it had happened. As I told him, he nodded his head again, smiled and looked at me as if the entire reason for his being on this site, this earth, had become clear to him, and said, 'You need some help with this?'

'Yes,' I said.

'I swap shifts at ten, then I'm free. I'll come get you and we'll do this.'

I could tell he was completely serious.

I felt my chin swelling up and becoming warm, but the rest of my body was cold so I put on the two electric heaters, and cleaned the drops of blood off my hands, the lid of Eugene's laptop and the floor and desks and chair, then sat, put my leg up, and texted Evelyn back. *Can't wait to see you! Still in at 7?*

And a few moments later she replied *Yes!*

Near the end of Evelyn's master's she had begun emailing me, from the library in Trinity College, links to a series of photographs showing the work of an artist from New York, who, during the seventies used to go to old abandoned structures in the city and cut out huge circular holes through the walls and floors, until you could see right through the building. This view was then photographed. One effect of this image was that it made bare to me the redundancy of the structure. I always thought it was a type of insanity what he was doing, like cutting off the branch of a tree you are sitting on. The photos looked so unseemly, but I always wanted to somehow pass through the space the holes made. Except for this, Evelyn almost never sent me material she was researching in university and I couldn't work out if it was because she was keeping it for herself until she felt confident enough to talk to me about it, or if I had shown an ambivalence to it at first and she didn't want to bother me again. I remember I emailed her back about this artist's work, he was called Gordon Matta-Clark, and I asked if we could go see these cut-up buildings sometime. She told me they were gone and the works mostly exist as photographs and, she said, the science of art history only happened because of photographs, and that although the photograph flattened art it also gave life to it; the photo made it possible to talk about an artwork without the thing being there. She often said that almost everything she knew about art comes from small pictures in books. I thought how this art-handling course she was doing must be thrusting her towards the objects of her study. I wondered if it was satisfying for her to hold and place someone else's artwork – something so distant and immediate and incomplete. Then, the first feeling of envy towards this new direction she was forging in her life appeared to me. It felt ugly, so I put the phone down, turned the mound of tissue paper in my hand and pressed it against my chin.

Jochen pulled the door open and squinted in. The rectangle of white light pouring out the door illuminated him sharply before dissipating into the dusk behind. His skin was pale and pink. He wore all black. Over his back was a green canvas bag with brass buckles, and every time he moved, the bag jangled with the empty plastic containers that held the protein shakes, fruit and nuts, and the raw meat he consumed in the security hut each day. As we walked down the ramp he asked me why I was limping, and when I told him, he chuckled, saying that I was not made for this place.

Once we got in to the lower ground floor I showed him the hole and he began laughing. He guffawed for ages. Then, wiping tears from his eyes, he gathered himself. He looked around at the collapsed ladders and the jackhammer and erupted again, and each time he looked at these things it seemed as though he was reconstructing the situation in his head anew; and each time he did this it seemed to become funnier to him and he would look from the gleaming sprawling ladders and the bits of concrete on the ground to the small dents in the wall, to my chin, to my face, and he would bend over with his hands on his knees as if he were about to throw up; he laughed, hooted and wheezed until he was making almost no sound at all, as if he were in some considerable pain and I thought that he might die. I would have laughed along with him but my mouth was sore. Then he coughed and dribbled. He wiped his eyes once more and chuckled to himself almost ruefully for a while, then he became serious and, shaking his head, picked the jack-hammer up and nodded, as if to acknowledge: okay, it is heavy, but it is okay.

He turned to me. 'Put a ladder beside the hole and hold it.'

He began breaking out the concrete. Soon he must have realized this would take longer than he thought and that it was not easy work, but he must also have known after laughing so abundantly at me that he would have to finish this job, or else he would never live it down, and not because I'd ever mention it to him, but for himself: there seemed to be no place for irony in his version of manliness, in his physical exertions, in how he ate, in his upkeep. He was muscular, but gym buff; his hands were soft and his bones were small. I wondered if he would stick it out.

An hour later Jochen had stripped to the waist and was cursing at the wall, the ladders, at me. He was sweating profusely. I said nothing. I looked at the ground and held the ladder as solidly as I could and prayed that none of our colleagues would walk in on this scene. By twelve o'clock Jochen had finished. He gave a small wedge of concrete one more hysterical blast from the jackhammer, like he was holding a machine gun over his head and the concrete chunk toppled. Then he threw the tool to the ground and began slapping the wall and jumping and whooping. He walked around beating his hairless chest, like he'd won some sort of bout, which in a way he had. I was relieved and thought how funny it would be if every worker celebrated like this each time they finished a job and how animated and individual and ecstatic the site would become.

As Jochen towelled himself down with his discarded T-shirt I realized that this was not work for him so much as a long, exotic workout. Then, as he put on his jumper, he said, 'We will go for a beer.'

We took a train to Schlesisches Tor and made our way under a bridge whose supports receded away with the

descending street lights and train line overhead. We entered
a pub with a dark smooth semicircular bar. In behind, cabi-
nets and mirrors and shadowy stained-timber shelves
extended up to the ceiling – an edifice of gin, vodka, whiskeys, schnapps and Fritz-kolas. The barman, who was in his
late forties, had sunken pebble-like eyes, and he leant against
the base of this cabinet, lighting a rollie. His wispy dark hair
was tied back in a samurai half ponytail. He advanced to the
bar as we did, smacked the top as he stood to attention in
front of us, looked me up and down, then looked to Jochen
and said, '*Yop?*'

Jochen ordered two Weissbiers. I could tell he and the
barman did not like each other. We sat in a far corner of the
bar and began drinking and I told Jochen about Evelyn and
me and where in Ireland we were from. He nodded and said
to me that he was originally from Frankfurt an der Oder,
over near the Polish border, and even though I did not ask,
he told me that he barely remembered the East because he
had been only three when the wall came down. I told him
about our old dog Pearl and about the day Evelyn and I first
found her, straggled and hungry, lying in a nook between a
rock and a piece of bog at the foothills of the Dublin mountains, a lead still on her. I told him about the notices we put
up on Facebook and all over town for weeks on end, and
hoping as the time passed that no one would come forward
to claim her. I told him about all of the time I spent with
her alone in the house, just after I'd been made redundant
from the last engineering consultancy I'd worked for, and

how I was sure her gentle company kept me from despair. As I recounted these simple stories his blue eyes softened in the most extraordinary manner, so I changed the subject in case I began crying too, and asked him where he worked out, because, I said, he was in seriously good shape.

He ignored my question and instead told me he often observed me on site. He said that it was strange for so passive a person that I didn't get taken advantage of more often. He reckoned this was on account of me being fair with people. I was unsure exactly what he meant, even a little weirded out at his silent attention. He then told me that he spent most of his twenties observing people while attempting to become a writer.

'You think I am a meathead, right?' he smiled.

I laughed.

He said he stopped writing after dedicating a year to reading Chekhov, consuming all the short stories and plays and becoming unhealthily obsessed. He told me that one day while reading 'The Lady with the Little Dog' he decided the only decent thing to do was to give up trying to be a writer. It was a tiny moment in the story, he said, where Gurov and Anna Sergeyevna are sitting on a bench, early one morning, on a promenade in Oreanda looking out over the Black Sea towards distant Yalta, after spending the night together. He told me that in this pause in their conversation, Chekhov describes their surroundings – the church behind them, the stillness of the air, the chirping cicadas, the mountains, the clouds, the wide skies, the monotonous hollow roar of the sea and the epic indifferent life force beyond all of this – until, Jochen said to me, a watchman comes along. With this Jochen drew closer and assured me that Chekhov was doing something extraordinary through Anna, and she back through him. His blue eyes, that were a few moments before wet with compassion, now flickered in heat. 'She,' he said, 'who was placed into this hugeness by Chekhov, then notices some dew on the grass in front of her. She,' Jochen whispered, pulling in so close that I could see nothing but his face, 'by drawing our attention to the dew and its smallness, makes the metaphoric hugeness around her larger than Chekhov could ever have intended and with the same stroke she completely obliterates it too.'

He sat back. 'It is the most beautiful moment in the world, and I will not ever forget it. I loved it the second I saw it, and I hated it too. So, the next week I began pumping iron, and I have not written since, and here I am now, years later, with you, drinking beer, and I think we should get some cigarettes.'

Out the window another swirl of snow descended as we drank, beer after beer, and within two hours we'd chain-smoked a pack of red Gauloises. We got another pack, then I suggested we speak in German but this went terribly and he asked if we could stop. I asked why. He said I was getting the genders of the nouns all wrong and it was hard for him to listen to. I became, for a moment, a little offended.

By four o'clock the bar had emptied and the barman was stacking stools onto the tables around us, so we left. When I stood outside again an icy wind gusted in from the east, and I remember almost nothing more except the musty smell of Jochen with his arm around me blackly leading me to the U-Bahn station.

I woke the next morning on his couch with all of my clothes on and a small pug dog sitting on my stomach staring at me. He barked, then jumped off and I peered around. Daylight streamed through the windows, filling the room, and I knew I was late for work. I fished my phone out and saw ten missed calls: nine from Gerald, one from Eugene and a text message from Gerald saying the hole in the lower ground floor wall was a disgrace and needed to be finished immediately. It was eight thirty. I left a message for Jochen on a piece of cardboard I'd ripped from a cereal box, thanking him for looking after me, and let myself out. When I stepped onto the footpath, the cold startled me. My head thumped. My throat was a tangle of briars and my knee throbbed, as if I had just fallen on it afresh. My jaw ached and I remembered my accident. I stopped the next person and asked where the nearest U-Bahn stop was. She was a tall blonde lady with a red beret and redder lips. I plotted my route along the slippery streets then down the steps of the U-Bahn station where a train pulled up, into which I slumped and dozed, allowing the train tracks to whizz along horizontally underneath and the carriage to fill and empty and fill and empty until it pulled into Alexanderplatz. I went for a coffee and croissant at the Italian café in the station. Then I had another.

The girl serving behind the bar was pretty, with an angular face and a high, dark and hastily made ponytail that swished around behind her as she took orders and made coffees and teas. Outside the broad café window I could see the bottom of the TV tower, its curved surface abstracted from the rest of the building. Sometimes the girl serving behind the counter would turn and the flails of her hair would cut across the line of the curve of the tower, creating brief Euclidean problems between the lines of her hair, the curve of her head and the larger, asymptotic curve of the tower base, and it seemed to me in those moments that she was completely aware of these fleeting geometric propositions she was putting before me but simply didn't care. I gazed at her. Then my stomach began turning against the second croissant and the two black coffees, the countless Weissbiers from the night before and the hole in the lower ground floor of the site. This ache built and churned, like a malignant ball and I felt, all of a sudden, extremely unwell, to the point of near panic. I paid the girl and stumbled, sweating, out of the café to the station toilets, rushed into a cubicle, stuck my fingers down my throat and threw up.

I sat on the toilet, mopped my brow and took out my phone: it was ten o'clock and I was so unaccountably late at this stage that it didn't matter if I took another hour. I went to the Galeria Kaufhof café at the top of the largest building in Alexanderplatz. I sat at an expansive window of what was probably once a very luxurious place and took in the views of the square, and the blocks of social housing proceeding east along Karl-Marx-Allee. I sipped cold sparkling water from a tall thin glass.

The first time I met Evelyn's parents was one autumnal Saturday afternoon in a busy café on the second floor of a department store in the middle of Dublin. We'd been going out for almost a year and she said her parents wanted to meet me. They had a grandparental air, or perhaps it was their fading aristocratic poise. They were both tall and trim. Harald was old but had a thick blaze of white hair and Elena's was straight with a light white-blonde going through it. They both had dark blue eyes but Evelyn's were more similar in tone to her father's. After a relaxing lunch, Elena and Evelyn left Harald and me in the coffee shop as they rambled off through the lower floors. Elena wanted to buy a new pair of walking shoes. Harald and I sat amid the clatter and hum of the café and conversed easily enough. He was a polite, softly spoken man, and as he sipped his glass of water he asked me a few questions about my work. We spent the rest of the time talking about some trips he took in the early fifties, as a young man, through southern Europe. He was basically a bum, he said, and he'd slept rough on beaches, under trees and on benches for ten months, seeing how well he could hide his German-ness, before he returned, exhausted, to his home near a town called Haßfurt in central Germany. Then he worked for years, grew to greatly dislike Germany and left in the late sixties with Elena to start a family in Ireland. He said he loved Ireland, particularly Leitrim, where he built his home. He said he loved Irish people. I listened with the sort of reverence a young man should reserve for a much older man when he is telling him a story about his life; one with no object or moral. He turned to me at one point and said, 'You know, Evelyn is a very private person.'

I didn't know what to say.

'She's quite like me, but is more fearless. I hope she's happy.'

'I think she is,' I said.

Later that evening after Evelyn came back from the train station, she told me that her parents had enjoyed my company and that Harald particularly liked my species of curiosity: he said my questions required many visual descriptions on his part and he liked that, because it forced him to remember.

I took another sip of water and peered down from the Galeria Kaufhof at the people darting across the square. Sitting at the table opposite were three enormous and heavily made-up women. They spoke Russian and were all in their sixties. They wore wide-brimmed hats and gold rings on their fingers and had thick dark eyeliner around their eyes. Their dresses and jackets seemed to alternate between leopard print, leather and fur, and these women were devouring enormous plates of food. It was utterly serene up there at that hour of the day and at that time of year. I was beginning to feel better. The grey day was lightening up again outside and I thought of the clamour and dust of the building site down below and considered not going in at all. I could call in sick, go home and get some rest before Evelyn arrived, because I wanted to enjoy chatting with her and I wanted to have sex intensely with her too.

Gerald appeared before me with a take-out coffee in his hand and I immediately realized how stupid I'd been in coming to this café. He always came here.

I looked up at him and he said, peering at my swollen chin, 'What happened to you?'

'Slipped on my way home.'

'Christ,' he said, 'you're having a bad run of it.' He looked at my glassy eyes, my clothes, my unwashed hair, my unshaven face – my aspect – and he decided not to pursue it.

'Eugene got that hole cleared up – it wasn't so bad in the end and the ducters are through it, but who broke it out? It's brutal.'

'Not sure,' I replied, 'I think one of the GOs.'

He shifted his weight. 'Have a coffee and some food. The clients aren't here for another twenty.'

'Grand,' I said, 'and did Franz get that copper back?'

'He did,' he said, 'the stones,' and he walked off.

Evelyn

The weekend before Evelyn left for her art-handling course in Cologne, we visited the Naturkundemuseum in the middle of the city. They were showing a touring exhibition, the centrepiece of which was a completely reassembled skeleton of a T-Rex, christened Tristan. Crowds milled around the place, with kids careering here and there, from cocooned animal to cocooned animal, to insect, to meteor, to bird. Evelyn and I detoured into the sea-life section of the museum where hundreds of fish and squid and small sharks were stacked in rows and rows that ran up to the ceiling, all of them yellowing in nineteenth-century jars. We ambled around the perimeter of this vaulted room for hours until the din in the outside halls fell away. There was so much to see, but I'd slumped into another banal Sunday evening depression. She was talking happily about her curatorial research and the exhibitions she'd lined up to visit the following week. I asked her if she'd mind if I took a break from work when we got to Cologne.

'Not at first,' I said, 'but eventually. Maybe just a couple of months.'

'You'll need one,' she said, a little surprised, 'Do you want to go somewhere?'

'No, but I think I'd like to do something else, sometimes I'd like to make something myself – a table with no top, a chair that's too high to sit on, something useless. I want to make it as well as I can, and destroy it afterwards; no one need even see it.'

'I'll help you figure this out, Paul,' she said.

We walked in silence for a while, then I turned to her again, and said, 'I just don't want to be left alone here without you.'

And her eyes welled up.

Earlier in the day we decided to go shopping for a new winter coat for Evelyn, but she could find nothing suitable. It was one of those rare Sundays during the year where department stores are permitted to open in Germany and I think this may have reminded her of home. It seemed to at once buoy and quieten her. Evelyn is a slim and neat person with narrow shoulders and dark and lustrous hair. It is the sort of hair that I think will never grey. And she has deep-set blue eyes and a handsome, clear and open face. She is even-tempered to the point, sometimes, of near illegibility. When I met her first she was working for the Central Bank, monitoring the vulnerabilities of international shadow-banking practices. She struck me as a diligent and able person – I thought she must have been a thorough economist too and a pleasant person to work with. She would wake early each morning, slip off to the kitchenette in our apartment, turn on the radio, make herself a pot of coffee and read the newspaper until I joined her. I never listened to the radio in the morning and I found these relaxing pre-work habits curious. After a year or two, the more she began to dislike, then grow to despise her work, the longer she'd spend in bed and that joyful part of the day, which seemed to be entirely in her make-up, disappeared and she would rise with me at eight, bring Pearl out for a quick walk and rush off to work. Then, almost out of the blue, she started evening classes in art history, and after a few weeks these blissful parts of her morning resumed. By the time she began her master's in art history she would rise early, often before dawn, make coffee and study or complete an assignment. Every Thursday she'd bake us something and I'd wake to the smell of a fresh cake circulating through the apartment, and think, *It's Thursday again.*

After a couple of months of seeing each other we were having sex without protection. I assumed she had gone on the pill and I was surprised one Saturday morning when I asked and she turned to me in bed and replied, 'Why would I put my body through that?' And because we both had jobs at the time I assumed if she became pregnant we'd just readjust and get on with it. After a year I asked her if she was worried about the lack of a child and she told me, 'No, it's fine. If it happens, it happens.'

She said this to me in a café one morning near the middle of town, and such was the carefreeness in her voice that I was tempted not to pursue it. 'I can get checked out,' I said.

'Don't,' she replied. 'Really, it's fine.'

I paused, then asked, bluntly, 'Is it you?'

'There's no reason why it should be,' she said, 'I'm healthy, you know.'

'Okay,' I said, 'only if you're sure. I don't mind going in.'

'It's entirely fine,' she said – she can sometimes sound remarkably posh, 'if it happens then great, if not, then that's great too. We can do other things.'

A few months later she called me from work telling me an old friend had asked her to be godmother to her child. She was the second friend to have contacted her about this kind of thing in little over a month. She'd turned them both down. Evelyn sounded, for the first time since I met her, properly flustered, even angry.

'Godmother, in this day and age?' she whispered.

When I first met Evelyn I quickly realized the extent to which she hated the Catholic Church: she'd often put down the newspaper or close her computer after reading another grim article about dead babies, or abused kids, or the numbers of women travelling for abortions, and say, 'The Pope, you know, he sits atop evil.'

She found anything that helped bolster the hold the Church had on the country to be a special sort of evil, 'An Irish evil,' she'd call it. 'An evil through intransigence,' she'd say.

'When I was in primary school,' she told me once, 'and because I wasn't christened, me and a small boy called Richard, who was Protestant, I think, spent every day, during the hour after lunch, on our own in the gym, waiting for religion class to end inside. It was the best hour of the day. He had spiky strawberry-blond hair and dark eyes, and he always wore cherry Docs. I think his father was a rocker or a roadie or something. For the whole of third and fourth year Richard and I would toy around in the gym, some days we'd kiss each other, over and over, and sometimes spend the time colouring in letters in our copy books, all of the 'o's and 'd's and 'b's and 'p's until the whole thing filled up into a sort of multicoloured musical composition. I told him that I loved him once. Then one day he didn't come to school and he didn't ever appear again, and I heard from a friend many years later that his father had had to return to England, and I often wondered what happened to him and where he lives now and what he might do. He was a lovely boy. For the rest of primary school, I was the only kid left sitting out in the gym during religion class, and I never cared about what was going on inside, it all seemed so pointless, like a man shouting at a field, and my parents never asked me about it either. But I felt like that gymnasium during those hours after lunch was a special part of Ireland, and I actually miss that place sometimes.'

The only time I've seen Evelyn cry in public was when we went to a screening of the old documentary *Rocky Road to Dublin* one wet summer's Sunday afternoon. It was at such an innocuous part of the film too, the bit where a priest walked around a country dance hall overseeing the young men and women as they tried to dance and express themselves. I saw, through the dark of the cinema, tears streaming down her face. And she didn't try to hide that she was crying – I always thought her evenness in public came from restraint, but though her expressions are muted, they are deep felt and, if appropriate, then fully expressed. My sense is that she finds Ireland a hysterical and insincere place. I think her ability to detach herself from it comes from her parents being German, being outsiders of sorts. Evelyn reckons that the only reason her parents were first accepted into the community in Leitrim was because they were German, and therefore the opposite of English. 'It's a welcome laced with hate,' she said to me once, 'and though I am fond of the place, I don't ever want to be part of it.'

I come from a large family where, when we were young, self-expression took on an at times exorbitantly competitive aspect, and I often wonder what the moulding forces on Evelyn, as an only child, might have felt like. In Evelyn's case her uniqueness in the family hasn't led to a sense of entitlement, more an easy ability for introspection, one, strangely, that is not self-consuming – it shows itself as quietness, or perhaps it is a gentle contentment with herself, one suggesting that she feels that being on the earth and busying yourself with something you more or less enjoy is sufficient, and there is enough sadness and great happiness to go around and eventually you will get a share of both. I am unsure at what register the fluxes of the world meet her, or trouble her, but she is calm and thoughtful company, and it hurts to imagine being without her.

In any case, to avoid having to attend these christenings, she decided we'd take our then annual holidays early, so we dropped Pearl down the country to my parents and left for ten days to a small lakeside house near a town called Sigtuna, about a hundred miles north of Stockholm. It snowed the whole time we were there. The house was at the foot of the most adamant set of mountains I've ever encountered. We got a taxi from Sigtuna train station with a quiet man who had a brown-blond moustache. He drove so slowly and wordlessly through the massive, glacial landscape that I guessed he must have been a very lonely sort of person. The house stood on its own on the shore along an inlet of a large lake and from the back garden the land rose steeply, curving upward to the sky. On our first morning I wandered outside to the garden with a mug of coffee in my hand, surveying this curve of land continuing up beyond some thick, low-lying tufts of grey cloud and I imagined this land mass bending in the sky into a giant loop that arced over the rumbling clouds then descended down behind me, crashing into the mountains on the other side of the lake. We hadn't planned our holiday but decided, at least, to bring books and food and drink and hibernate in the house – and take short walks in this wilderness. After a few days a melancholy overcame us both and we were unable to spend any time in one space together. Whenever I'd enter a room Evelyn would leave within a few minutes, and when I went to join her she'd go again. We spent one day almost completely separate, sometimes meeting wordlessly in the dark corridors of the cottage, or in the kitchen. At night we slept without touching. The lake to the front of the house was completely frozen over but we barely ventured outside.

At the start of the second week I said to Evelyn that the mountains were too big, the place was making me feel down and that I wanted to go back to Stockholm and be among people. In Stockholm we stayed in a hotel with a large skating rink whose roof consisted of substantial timber rafters; as if a beached whale had frozen itself into the ground, become desiccated and its ribcage had been covered over again to house these many atom-like skaters whizzing frivolously about on the rhomboidal white plane below. Evelyn brought me out to skate but I was tentative; I did not want her to see me fall. I thought that if I fell in front of her I would smash into millions of pieces. She insisted, but the sense of imbalance agitated me and I took myself off the rink, stood at the barrier and watched her complete two leisurely loops. Later that evening over some drinks she said that her dad had taught her how to skate and that he was an excellent skater and it was the one thing he missed about Germany, especially during the milder winters in Ireland. She told me about one winter morning when she was in her early teens, it had been particularly cold that year, and the small oxbow lake at the foot of the hill near their house was completely frozen over. She'd risen just after dawn, and made her way down to the sitting room. The surrounding fields and hedge-rows were entirely white and she saw, through the naked and crystalline beech and birch trees fronting the boundary of her house, her father, in a short grey jacket and a dark cap, gracefully skating on the bright lake below, swerving around in s-shapes, then pushing himself off in another direction, his hands behind his back. He would gently brake with the toe, scraping the surface of the ice behind him, then he'd accelerate off into another direction, his knees bending beneath him, and she said that she was stunned that morning looking at him skating across the small hardened lake because he looked so alien and so happy and it occurred to her how suddenly he could disappear. She said that was all she could think about in that house on the lake near Sigtuna.

2.5 *Rocks and men*

By the time I got down from the café to site, Eugene, the Ukrainian engineer, was in the cabin sitting on his own. It was almost twelve o'clock and the day was warming up a little. The sun had at last broken through the monoliths of cloud that had seemed to sit over Berlin for the entirety of the previous three months. The top crust of hardened slush and snow was melting and the streets glowed silver. I could do an hour or two of work, but when I'd eat again later in the day the energy for digestion would most likely floor me. I was a rolling fulcrum for my own bodily functions.

Eugene inquired about my chin and I told him the whole story. He chuckled and said I should've called him, he would have happily helped out because he did little with his evenings here. He had my notebook opened out in front of him. I was embarrassed because he was looking at the 'Love notes' section, so I slid it back across the table towards me, powered up my laptop and pulled on my boots.

As I put on my site vest he nudged my elbow with his, turned his screen and said, 'That's me, there. Can you see?'

It was a scan of a black-and-white photograph of him, as a much younger man, with a fit physique, about to dive from a rowing boat into a body of water that looked to be the inlet of a lake. The water was rippling smoothly in the foreground, his toes were still touching the side of the boat and his body was almost completely unfurled into an arch. I imagined, in the next moment, the water being smashed, the boat rocking back and forth, and him, appearing a few seconds later like an otter, breaking the surface of the water farther up the lake.

'That's me and my college friends,' he said, 'we were at a labour camp for summer break. We did nothing, absolutely nothing.'

I smiled. His accent was very Russian: he rolled all of his 'r's, dipped deeply into his 'u's and his 'o's were flat. He clicked to another photo of him and these friends sitting on ploughed-up rows of earth in the middle of a dark field. The furrows led off out of the picture to a distant, long-gone perspective point, and behind the field were low-slung farm buildings with a trail of people approaching them. He was in the middle of the frame, smoking a cigarette and smiling and he looked as though he was about to say something to the person taking the picture.

'Nothing,' he said, 'absolutely nothing, even when we were working we did nothing.'

'What year is this?' I asked.

The photos looked like something from the turn of the last century.

'Summer 1982.'

'Wow.'

He looked at me, smiled and nodded. 'Yes, nothing.'

The next photograph showed an attractive young woman in what looked like a bridal outfit. She was gazing to the right-hand side of the photographer and the framing had clipped her feet off.

'My wife,' he said, 'on our wedding day,' and he scrolled to the next photo, which showed them standing together beside a large concrete bridge support, alongside a glittering river. She was grasping a bouquet of flowers and had smaller flowers arranged around her headband, and he wore a pale-coloured suit. He stood to her right with his left arm around her slim waist, and his other hand reaching over to rest on hers. They were both smiling and his left eye was half closed, but they were a handsome couple, of good proportions.

'We got married beside that bridge,' he said, 'on a beautiful day. The bridge was new. In her village, this is a custom: all newly married couples that year had their ceremonies beside this bridge.'

'Where are you from?' I asked.

'I grew up near the top of the Ural mountains,' he said, and he made a mound shape with the tips of the fingers. 'A small village too, but not as small as Varvara's. I left when I was sixteen; I went to study engineering in Moscow. I liked motorbikes and tennis and swimming and girls,' he said as he clicked the mouse, 'and then I met Varvara,' and he nudged me again, 'now look,' and he gestured to another photo, taken from a height, and on the ground below were eight slim young men, stripped to their waists lying in the sun, across a pile of rocks, all of which were a little bigger than their chests. The whole picture was rocks – rocks and men, no buildings, no trees, no rivers.

'Another summer my college mates and I had to go to Siberia. We spent all of July and August moving this mound of rocks from one part of the valley to another, about fifty metres away, completely unnecessary,' he said, 'the train embankment was never built.' He looked to the screen, then back at me. 'And this is us on the last day,' he said, 'lying on our rocks,' and he began laughing – a strange succession of hiccups that shook his shoulders up and down. He looked over to me laughing like this, then at the photograph, then back at me, and eventually, so infectious was this odd laugh and his arched eyebrows that I was compelled to laugh also. I laughed for some time, then buried my face in my hands. Then I stopped, coughed, and Eugene swivelled to his desk. I sat back in my chair and stifled a yawn. I decided to shake off the tiredness and left for the site.

I wandered in through the rear entrance of the ground floor. Two plasterers, all in white, leaned onto a railing over-looking the lift pit. Their backs were to me and they resem-bled Grecian sculptures, but with their heads chopped off. One of them, a man in his mid-thirties turned. He had dark hair, and once I caught his eye, he beckoned me over.

'*So Mann, mein Chef hat gesagt, dass er uns nicht bezahlen kann.*'

'*Wie bitte?*' I said, I was far too tired to compute.

'*Unser Chef, mein Boss, er hat gesagt,*' he said, pointing to his mouth, '*dass er unser Geld nicht auszahlen kann,*' he continued, rubbing his fingers together to indicate money.

'*Geld?*'

'*Ja, Bezahlung,*' he scoffed. '*Unser Chef kann uns nicht auszahlen, wenn ihr Scheisser ihn nicht bezahlt.*'

'*Kann nicht verstehen,*' I said, shaking my head.

'*Scheisse, du konntest gestern gut sprechen, wenn du etwas von uns willst, du Scheisser,*' he said, suggesting I could understand him only when it suited.

'*Ich kann mit Ihrem Boss sprechen, wenn dass hilfreich ist?*' I said, merely coagulating stock phrases, offering him vague promises of help.

They turned back to the lift shaft, and the man I had spoken to spat into the pit. I moved away. Whenever I managed a conversation in German it lifted my spirits, just so also, when I couldn't, it made me feel quite dumb.

By the time I got to the lower ground floor it was almost one o'clock, coming up to lunch, and the place was folding down from a manic buzz into a slower, easier pace. I was suddenly wrecked and had to lie down – the whole floor revolved around me. I made my way to the basement, which was all but empty. I shuffled down a new corridor to the rear corner of the building. A painter rolled white emulsion out onto the walls. He'd an MP3 player at his feet, emitting tinny trad music. I wished the whole place would go black again, and empty and cold, for a day or just for a few hours so as I could get some rest. I rounded a corner and went into the first aid room. The light pinged on overhead. Having locked the door, I lay on the bench, closed my eyes, balled my high-vis under my head and began to breathe slowly. As the light overhead went out, I sank into the small darkness that surrounded me: my eyes twitched as my breathing deepened and I could feel my heart slacken.

Then I fell asleep, or fell so close to sleep that a series of lucidly limber and disconnected images began to form in my mind, things that took no effort of mine to appear, things like dreams, but not my dreams and I am not sure if this really happened, but as I lay in the cold darkness of the basement — below the city's water table with its intimate subterranean admixtures of churning soil, stones, bones, chemicals and water — I began to hear what seemed to me like Russian folk music and I imagined I was curled up, slopping around, in the womb of an enormous Russian woman. I imagined the person playing this music was my father, fifty years ago, in a small house, with a crackling fire, in the sylvan depths of a cold, white, muffled winter. I thought of Eugene, my older brother, sitting on the ground, on the other side of my mother's womb, toying with wooden blocks, and how much fun we would have growing up together, but also how sad I would be when he'd leave us for his military service, then college, then work, then marriage, and how lonely my mother and father will be the day he goes and how quiet the house will become without him, but mostly, I thought twice from my mother's womb, how much I will miss our games of badminton in early summer on the very clear days, with the chill still not fully chased from the air and the momentary lines and arcs that the shuttlecocks make in the sky as we bat them over and back to each other, like small Exocets careering then correcting themselves in the air, then swirling tinily in the erratic breezes of the Urals, down, down and landing at my feet; and I, despondent, looking up at my lithe, handsome older brother obscured by the net crumpling and reforming and tautening across his face, torso, thighs, and the mountainous landscape behind and he hopping up and down twirling his badminton racket in his hands as he crows and celebrates with wind-whipped shouts, proclaiming over and over again, 'Inwevitable, inwevitable, inwevitable!'

I started, shook my head and got off the bench. The light flickered on above me and I shuffled up the corridor and opened another door. More lights came on. I pulled a rectangle of cardboard out of a sink, turned on the tap, and to my surprise water flowed. It was cold. I splashed my face ten, fifteen times, until I eventually came to. It was a quarter to three, so I went back up to the lower ground floor and waited for the visiting executives to arrive – to join the entourage, answer any questions they might pose, and describe progress with an appropriately humble confidence.

The three executives came late and we didn't finish until six. There was no time to go home, shower or clean up before meeting Evelyn. I left site, took the U-Bahn to Eberswalder Strasse and waited for her outside.

A note on pedestals

Site hoardings are odd things. They sometimes consist of galvanized fences chained together around a site, upon which are sometimes hung signs and whatnot, but you can peer in through them at the work proceeding. More often the site hoarding is made up of seven-foot-high panels of timber where advertising space is rented out. It is difficult to see over them.

When the hoarding around our site was dismantled, and our building, at last, directly addressed the public footpaths and roads surrounding us, it was as if a pedestal that had held the building site aloft had been collapsed, removed, and the small secrets of the site's brief life were laid bare too. It occurred to me as we did this that the finished building seemed less and less the point of the building site. The completed building was merely the building site's exhaust.

A note on the look of complication

Complicated systems in static structures are ones made up of many simple elements, but it is their sheer numbers that make a complicated system difficult to understand; whereas fluids are complex systems and even at their simplest are unstable and difficult to grasp.

I always thought the look of structural engineering had a bias for, or even a love of, complication, but not of complexity, and that this appreciation of the complicated was a look that those outside the trade could not see, were not shown, or were not interested in; but this look lies dormant in engineers too, particularly structural engineers because their appreciation of the complicated isn't totally graphic: it is an appreciation that sits, at first, in their habits of imagining, where a problem is located, stilled, magnified, then extracted from the complicated scenario down to a simpler one, where it can then be analysed and understood, then bent back into the world of material strengths, ductilities, stiffnesses and practical applications. And the great fault of engineering, its ultimate deductive fallibility, is when it turns this habit of thinking towards complex and fluid things. Engineering tries to make complex things complicated first, and only then does it enact its method; and this, I realize, is a type of madness, and though convincingly useful in many ways, it is also a habit of thinking that is spiritually eviscerating in its limitations, and only a few great engineers can use this habit to its full while also holding it at bay so as they can imagine beyond it, or see through it, as it were.

2.6 *Systems of art*

It began snowing as I stood waiting at the foot of the U-Bahn station. The floating rhombus flakes took on a green orangeness as they drifted down below the streetlights like thousands of tiny kites, before they were lost to the ground. My gaze shifted from the scaffolding across the way up to the steps of the station. Evelyn was there, struggling down the stairs, her suitcase in both hands. She looked beautiful, and was smiling broadly by the time she got to the ground. I pulled her to me and we kissed and I told her how much I'd missed her and how happy I was that she was back. As we hugged I felt her head leaning against the side of mine, and her hands gathering clumsily on my back, pulling me together tight, and I gazed, for what felt like an age, at the slush on the street shining green then red.

The smell of her.

We were freezing and quickly found a bar a few corners away. It was dark and smoky. We sat at a stout candlelit table at the back of it. She took her hat off. Her hair was cut up short.

'What do you think?'

'I love it,' I said, and leaned forward to ruffle it, 'when did you get it done?'

'A week back. I was nervous – it's never been this short. Do you really like it?'

'I do, I love it. You look great. Same can't be said for me, but ...'

She laughed at my chin and straight out guffawed when I told her how it happened. She said I looked wrecked, so I told her about the hole, Jochen, the pints the night before and my morning, to which she mock-cried.

I went to the bar as she took off her coat and gloves and I got us a couple of beers. I gave her a kiss on the cheek, which was still cold. I sat back down and said, 'So, you can handle art!'

She rolled her eyes and smiled. 'It was great; I met everyone. They're really nice,' she said, 'they gave me a tour of the offices and all. The gallery's in an old part of the city, surrounded by lovely cobbled streets and, y'know, august buildings. It's amazing. It was a church once but they extended it years ago, some big-name architect, and the sound through the exhibition hall, when it's empty, is like standing inside a bell.' She toyed with a beer mat. 'And my boss, Katrin, told me she was delighted to have me on board.' Then Evelyn paused, 'I'm blathering,' and smiled again, then looked at me and said, as she leaned forward and touched my face, 'I think this will work. I think we'll be okay.'

She then described the first project she'd begin in August, and how extensive it was and how it was all going towards an exhibition the following September on minimalist art. She told me that she'd become totally immersed in it. She took out her phone and flicked through images of these minimalist works: all shiny steel boxes, white cube frames and pared-back forms and lines.

'They were all American dudes,' she said, 'and they used these empty warehouses and factories during the fifties and sixties to develop their look.'

She told me about a state collection she visited in Cologne during her stay and how, as she was guided through the collection, she came upon an artwork by Donald Judd, a small plexiglass and steel cuboid that she had seen countless times during her studies, on slides, in lectures or in books, but when she encountered it, sitting on the floor in front of her, she was shocked at how small and quiet the piece was, and how it did away with things like composition and previous expressions of time. She smiled as she took a sip from her beer, 'It's valuable, you know – it costs a lot – but it has artistic value too, and for work like that it is impossible to disentangle them, and one type of value is no more noble than the other, I don't think anymore,' she said, with no hint of nostalgia. She told me she cared less and less about the contemporary fashions in art, but that she was more inter-ested in the complexity of the whole thing and that it was a world she would always find challenging, no matter how solid or singular an artwork or era appeared.

As she spoke about these different systems of art I realized that with this new career in Cologne, Evelyn was moving into a world that was complex and unstable, a world far more exhausting, frustrating and challenging than the world I worked in. She had the joy, I thought, to not just focus on but also turn away from the swerving and, to me, mysterious currents of art. I reckoned too, sitting with her drinking our beers, that she would have a splendid working life.

I told her that I thought she was daring.

She stopped playing with her beermat and replied, 'It's not daring, I don't think, doing something that you want to do. If you want to do it then there's no bravery, it's just will. The hardest thing, though, is finding what it is, you know? I hope everyone could find out what it is they like to do. I wish everyone could be as happy as I am.'

I suggested we buy some cigarettes and as the pub filled around us she told me about some locales where we might live in Cologne and the sort of rents these different areas were making. As we chatted, we became more excited at the prospect of moving there and my energy surged and I forgot I was tired, and we drank, beer after beer, clinking the butt of the glasses each time, and we got very drunk, both very quickly and we smoked cigarettes, one after another, together in the back room of this curious, rustic German bar that was playing death-metal music quietly and had perfectly arranged candles dotted around the back spaces, throwing just enough light upon everything in the room. It occurred to me that it didn't matter if we never made it to

Cologne, because hoping about life, however briefly, with another person is enough.

A candle fluttered, casting sea-shook shadows on the walls. Then another went out and it seemed as if that part of the room had suddenly fallen away into an almighty abyss. Then we kissed again and drank and smoked some more. We soon realized it was late and we were both slurring our words so we got a taxi home and went straight to our bedroom. I took all of her clothes off and she stood naked in front of me in the half light. I had all of my clothes still on – my boots, and my dressy woollen jacket. I could feel her waist and her thighs. She opened the front of my trousers and I pulled her towards me and I moved her onto me and we fucked against the wall. Then she took me onto our bed and I knew that we were going to go into the position we used to always fuck in when we met first, me on my knees and Evelyn on top of me, sitting down on me and we would rock slowly then faster and I would try to hold off so as we could come together. But my knee was in agony; when it hit the bed, I winced, and Evelyn asked me if I was okay. I said I was, and knelt on the bed with my cock sticking out of my trousers, and my dressy woollen jacket falling down behind me. It was as if she was about to have sex with a small bear. She climbed onto me and I grabbed her and she put her legs around me and when she lowered herself onto me I shifted the weight to my left knee, hoping the pain would stop me from coming. We kissed intensely and moved with each other four, five times and she caught her breath and I guessed that she had either come or that she had realized she was too drunk to do so, because she had gone limp on top of me and she began gently kissing the side of my neck and I started to fuck her, or at least I started to fuck against the feeling at the top and underside of my cock and I felt a panic rising in me, which had begun to develop in my early thirties when my heart would start pounding very hard whenever I had sex in this position, me carrying Evelyn. I began to thrust frantically, sensing that either I or Evelyn were coming apart. I was in a race with my clattering heart before it gave out. Then the searing pain in my left knee was subsumed into the intensity of the ecstasy in the rest of my body. I began to gasp, I would say, because I had beaten my heart to it once more. I pulled her hips towards me as hard as I could and bucked and came hard and long three times, then I thrust once more, as if I was trying to come out through Evelyn altogether and in that moment my knee, the extraordinary pain in my knee grew and began appearing to me very clearly, and my heart, I was sure was going far far too hard and fast and I thought that this was it, that my heart was going to finally crack. Then I threw Evelyn off me, gasped, and fell back. She was startled. I straightened out my leg in front of me and grabbed at the joint with both hands and winced, then grabbed at my chest and tried to take my jacket off and open my shirt. I gulped for breath, for some control, and pulled at my shirt buttons and looked around me, but I could see nothing. Then I felt her hand on my chest and I calmed a little and very slowly my heart and my lungs and my knee started to settle, bob and subside. Evelyn was sitting up beside me, looking down. She asked if I was okay. I took deep, careful breaths. I put my right hand around her waist and pulled her down towards me. She laid her head onto my chest, on the breast pocket of my jacket. My breathing slowed and I could smell a mixture of floral shampoo and smoke off her hair. I fell asleep, then woke up in the early hours of the morning. Evelyn was in bed beside me breathing evenly, under the covers, and I was lying on top of the covers with all of my clothes still on. I got up, undressed, turned my phone off and got into the bed beside her. I felt her naked body near me. We embraced, and it was like I had plunged headlong with her into a deep black midsummer bog hole; and I thought that I could stay here, in this smell, in this extraordinary warmth, in this dark, for a very long time.

Love note 4

der Rausch – intoxication

rauschen – to roar, to murmur, to rustle, to hiss, to flutter

> *Es rauschen die Wipfel und schauern,*
> *Als machten zu dieser Stund'*
> *Um die halb versunkenen Mauern*
> *Die alten Götter die Rund.*

> The treetops rustle and shudder
> As if at this very hour
> The ancient Gods
> Were pacing these half-sunken walls.

> Joseph von Eichendorff, '*Schöne*
> *Fremde*' ('Beautiful Stranger')

2.7 East, west and somewhere else

Next morning, I woke to the smell of coffee. Outside, low knots of cloud slid by. It was snowing gently. The light was not bright, nor dark – it was oscillating, vibrating between night and day. Evelyn came in carrying a small pink cup and saucer we'd bought at a Christmas market a few months before. I sat up. She joined me on the side of the bed and handed me the coffee. Then she placed the back of her hand against my chest and ran it down my stomach. We looked to each other as she slipped her hand under the covers. I was aware of the cup of hot coffee. She smiled at me. Her face was soft angles of falling shadow and light. Her dark hair, boyish, raffish. She looked me up and down and continued to say nothing. I became hard and she wanked me once, twice, three times. Then she stood and walked back to the door, removing her T-shirt as she went. She was wearing a pair of my boxer shorts and she knew this irritated me no end. She was in one of her funny moods. She turned and stood for a moment at the door, looking down at me.

'*Komm mal, a ladeen*,' she said – she was on the edge of smiling, 'we'll go out now for a walk.'

An hour later we were huddled together making our way through the snow towards Bornholmer Brücke, an old steel bridge that was once split in two by the wall. It was shrouded in scaffold. We walked from east to west stopping at the top to gaze down on the city sprawling before us. In the foreground fields of power lines and railway tracks criss-crossed and swerved through the land, edged out by low-rise pastel-coloured *altbau* apartments feeding south, into the thickening swirls of intermingling snow and fog and cloud settling over the middle of the city. Way above, the tiny red lights halfway up the TV tower throbbed wanly until they disappeared completely. We continued on west into Wedding. Evelyn was buoyant, sometimes breaking into a skip beside me. Parents were pulling children in timber sleds along footpaths, all of them heading to the nearest incline. Their breaths puffed out before them cartoonishly, and the street echoed with shrieks and cries. We followed the hordes into a playground where there was a hill with scores of kids whizzing effortlessly down the broad slope.

We stopped for a moment and surveyed the savagery.

'That hill there, it's made from building rubble,' Evelyn said, turning to me, 'some old guy got talking to me here one day, a Herr Dudek, I think it was. He was thin. He was so thin I thought he'd crumple in front of me. He told me the hill was made from the rubble of buildings around here that had been wrecked during the war. He must have been bored because he hung around for ages telling me how he'd once worked for the Stasi, but when the wall came down he moved to Wedding because his house, which was back east, was being bombarded with hate mail and his front door vandalized by ex-prisoners. Crazy, no?' and she rubbed her nose with the back of her hand. 'He said the last straw was when they made a museum out of the prison he'd worked in for years. He was so angry that he'd often visit just to stage his own one-man protest. One day, he met an ex-prisoner he'd once roughed up. The man seized Herr Dudek in the foyer of the museum and beat him up so badly that he lost consciousness and had to get his jaw reset. He pressed charges and all, and won, and his assailant did more time, and old Dudek said there are ways for dealing with things and this man, this ex-prisoner had taken matters into his own hands, and that was unfair, he told me.'

'Christ,' I said.

'I know.'

She put her hands on her hips and stood almost dynamically in the breeze. The blue bobble on her hat shook. Her nose was red and moist. She sniffled again, and her breath plumed. I was wrapped in a woollen jacket and a thick white scarf. We clasped our gloved hands clumsily and headed back onto the main drag towards Wedding.

After another half hour we stopped in a busy Turkish café for an omelette and a black tea. Then we set off south-east again. We hadn't been to this part of town before so we just wandered around the streets, getting lost and seeing what might appear to us.

We ventured down one street lined with second-hand clothes and furniture shops, slowing as we passed each window. We'd call in the odd time to rummage for nothing in particular. Evelyn had begun collecting small books produced by Reclam of Leipzig. There seemed to be thousands of these attractive pocket books around Berlin, but Evelyn only chose ones that were ancient. She'd analyse the binding of each book and the old gothic font, the near-translucent paper, then the cover, turning the small delicate thing over in her hands, deep in concentration. Before she'd decide on whether to purchase or not, she'd open the book out and take a theatrical smell of the pages, then, happy, she'd haggle with the shopkeeper or stall owner about getting the thing down a bob or two from what I thought was already a pretty meagre price. She had an expanding collection of translations of Shakespeare plays already arranged on a shelf in the apartment, each in different states of repair. Sometimes, on a Sunday evening, she'd read them. She liked *Macbeth* because she'd studied it in school, as had I. She said she loved reading the German version of the text; the images from reading this version, she said, sat on the English version she remembered, like dust from a twice shaken-out blanket.

We stopped at a junction. A tram eased by. We kissed, then wandered down another street and another, all of which had names like Amp, Volta, Watt. A massive Siemens building loomed up before us. Evelyn burst out laughing, turned, grabbed my hand and we ran away. We arrived in another park, this time full of trees covered over in snow. The place was empty.

'Where the fuck is everyone?' she said.

It was so still and quiet that I was afraid if we moved too quickly or did something too abrupt we'd trigger an avalanche of the snow resting on the hundreds of frail branches of trees around us and we'd be engulfed. I imagined Evelyn and I buried in snow together, many feet from the surface, looking at each other in a wan blue-white light, both of us a breath from panic.

We came out of the park and headed to a dimly lit corner bar across the way and had hot chocolates. I asked the owner if he had a painkiller; my head had begun to thump. He didn't, so instead I ordered a whiskey.

'Whiskey and hot chocolate, together at last,' Evelyn beamed when I arrived back down to the table. She went to the bar and got one too.

We drank our whiskeys and our hot chocolates. The street lamps rustled to life outside as the dark enveloped them.

'Are we old?' she asked me.

'Dunno,' I said.

'I feel old,' she said.

'Maybe you feel tired,' I replied, 'I feel tired.'

We had another whiskey then left.

It was becoming extremely cold. The snowing had ceased and the clouds were dissipating. The sky became a giant clearing of stars. The fresh falls of snow that day were hardening and becoming slippy. Each footstep crunched loudly – the mass decimation of crystals. It was as if, in this part of town, so untouched was the snow that it seemed no one had ventured from their house all day. We continued along some streets turning left, then right, deciding to walk down a road merely on the basis of how it was lit and whether there was the possibility of a forgotten pub on the street, or a bar, or a *Kneipe* where some old German person might tell us some secret about the place. We passed a small pub, called simply 'Small Pub'. Inside, three men were perched around the bar smoking a spliff and drinking bottles of beer. There were no taps, just a barman, sozzled drunk, sipping wine and honking occasionally on the spliff that was being gently passed around. We ordered two beers and sat at a table across the way and looked at the quiet carriageway outside. The barman appeared beside us, offering, *'Möchtet ihr kleines Toke?'* and we took some, then passed it on to the man who would have been next, had we not arrived. They smiled and, after I don't know how long, we both felt pretty stoned. Then a man who had a small black border collie came over. He was opening a plastic tub full of meatballs. He offered us some. We took one each and ate. They were so freshly made that in the centre the meat and onion was still warm. They were the most delicious thing I've ever tasted. We entered a fine state of bliss, headiness and fatigue. We said nothing for a long time. All we could hear was the odd mutter or chesty laugh from the bar, the thump of a glass being placed on a towel on the counter and the dog yawning and stretching. Then the hound wandered over to us, sniffed our feet, and Evelyn stroked his head with one hand while playing with the candle wax with her other. I put my hand on her thigh. She looked to me. Her face was completely expressionless, and she said exactly nothing.

We left, waving goodbye to the men and walked back out onto the street. The cold was by then, incredible. The wind was back up and the sky was clouded over again. We huddled together and walked, bouncing off each other for miles, left, then right, then right again, then left – the snow, all the while, falling in garbled drifts. We walked and walked wordlessly into the whiteness, until I could not feel Evelyn any more, or see her, smell her, or hear her and I was suddenly alone on another strange street, embracing the elusive, digressing snow.

Next morning it was Sunday and Evelyn was nudging me awake. I came to and she produced her phone, showing a photograph of four small timber sculptures.

'Matthew, Mark, Luke and John,' she said, turning to me.

I squinted at them.

'We're going to see them today,' she continued.

I tried to fall back to sleep, but she was already up and noisily getting herself together. She stalked over and back across the end of the bedroom and out to the bathroom and back again. I can tell by how she walks in the morning if she wants me to get up or not. If she walks on her heels at all, it means, without her saying anything, *Get up to fuck, Paul*.

We arrived down at the Bode Museum in the middle of the city at around noon. The sun was back out and the snow from the previous day was thawing. The waste-water gutters gurgled orchestrally. We stopped for a coffee in a tourist café along by the shore of the Spree and then went to the museum on the other end of the island.

We strolled through the building looking at the old paintings and sculptures until we came to the four unpainted wooden sculptures of the evangelist saints Evelyn had shown me in bed. They were arranged at the back of a room filled with other diminutive wooden sculptures. Over the years I'd seen lots of marble and plaster sculptures in various museums in Dublin and London, but I don't think I'd ever seen wooden ones like this before. They were odd things, toy-like, and their heads looked a little too large. Their delicacy was new to me. The four saints stood there with their backs to the wall, their facial expressions relaying anxiety, sadness, reticence and doubt, or a mixture of all four in each. Evelyn took a seat on the bench in front of them and opened her notebooks. I knew she'd be here for a while examining the sculptures, so I decided to wander through the neighbouring rooms taking in the rest of the wooden universe.

Near the back of the next room, on a steel plinth, sat another timber sculpture, about two foot tall, of Saint George slaying a dragon. What a curious thing. The dragon looked more like a demon dog than the enormous scaly beast

I'd always imagined. It was twisted around the feet of Saint George's horse. It looked to be injured, or at least in some distress, mid-scream even, while the horse's face was stern, almost sullen, and looking in a different direction to the creature below, and then Saint George's face – he decked out in armour that seemed to have stolen the scales from the beast at his horse's feet – was utterly serene, even morose, sickly, his eyes averted to another place again, but downward. It was one of the saddest faces I have ever seen, and made no sense at all with the high drama he was seemingly caught up in, his sword above his head ready and waiting to strike and slay the strange animal flailing on the ground beneath. I walked around to the back of the sculpture and, where Saint George's knee plunges into the flank of his horse, I noted a rash of imperfection in the otherwise perfectly smooth wood. That was where a knot in the lime tree must once have been located, and I saw where the sculptor had struggled expertly around the flaw. I circled back towards the front of the object, now engrossed in the oddness of it, its size, neither figurine, nor statue, nor puppet, nor icon, nor plaything – all three creatures hewn from the one chunk of wood, and perhaps it was their inseparability that saddened Saint George so, his face was one of a person trapped forever illustrating an unwanted duty. I inspected the cracks around the bodies of the three creatures – myth, scaffold and man – and I noticed in the neck of the dragon a particularly large cut, but I could not tell if this was an imperfection, or some damage with age, or if it was a cut put there by the sculptor implicating this unhappy Saint George in its violence. Then I noticed the sign at the base of the plinth: *Bitte nicht berühen!* and I thought, Saint George would probably like nothing more than to be touched, and disturbed from the exhaustion of his duty. I circled the thing a few more times, then with an overwhelming urge to pick it up, or at least to touch it, I decided to walk back out to the four saints. Evelyn was already gone.

Pearl

In Dublin, during the fledgling late autumn days, when I was first out of work, I would go with Pearl to the park near our apartment and throw a blue rubber ball for her. She loved that ball. It became one of the best parts of those jobless days for me, with the different rhythms, dynamics and rates of movement, retraction and intention, between my mind, my arm, the ball, Pearl's darting runs, the last few yellow leaves dropping in curves from the trees around us, the ball brought to a stillness in Pearl's mouth and with it the sudden casting up of the dried-out leaves from the ground into the air around Pearl's dark, twisting body; then, her aimless trot back to me, to drop the ball at my feet again, for me to pick up and throw once more. In those idle times I spent with her everything was reduced to hapless rhythms, and the guilt of being out of work and being behind on many different bill and bank repayments fell away into unimportance. When I did not throw the ball, Pearl would stop amid the leaves and stare seriously at me. She'd stand to attention for a while, then sit, lick her lips, then lie, and in the silence that grew between us it felt as though we were occupying separate points in two altogether different universes, one where the passing of time had no consequence, the other, where it had a little less.

Part 3

May

Hold, while Prometheus is about it, I'll order a complete man after a desirable pattern. Imprimis, fifty feet high in his socks; then, chest modelled after the Thames Tunnel; then, legs with roots for 'em, to stay in one place; then, arms three feet through the wrist; no heart at all, brass forehead, and about a quarter of an acre of fine brains; and let me see – shall I order eyes to see outwards? No, but put a sky-light on top of his head to illuminate inwards. There, take the order, and away.

Herman Melville, *Moby-Dick*

A note on types of engineering student

I realized recently that there are four types of engineering student: the hardworking but limited student; those with photographic memories (who are usually strong mathematicians); the intuitively brilliant (who usually made good designers); and a blend of the last two.

I was of the first variety, and you often found types from the following two. Though the fourth type was rare, I knew one – he was called Neil. In first year in university in Belfast I used to drop over to his apartment the night before our end-of-term exams. He'd be reclined on his leatherette sofa, watching TV, smoking a spliff and drinking tea from a stained Leeds United mug. He was a laid-back person with thin straggly hair. He wore steel-rimmed glasses, was a little overweight and always dressed in black jeans, boots and a long, dark coat; and he only ever wore Metallica T-shirts. He smelled a little, but either didn't notice or simply did not care, and his presence the night before exams at first helped me relax, but by fourth year I had stopped calling over because his pre-exam calmness just highlighted the yawning intellectual chasm between us, which instead of composing me before my final-year exams, pulled me into a deep feeling of boundedness.

At first we used to go drinking together at the weekends and Wednesday evenings after five-a-side football games. By third year he'd chosen mechanical engineering whereas I went with structures and we didn't see each other so much after that because we were always meeting separate deadlines and the parts of the faculty we were based in were at different locations in the campus.

I bumped into him once near the end of February in our last year as we were nearing the end of our theses projects. He was walking towards the fluids lab where he was conducting his experiments. He asked me to join him. We chatted amiably as he led me down to the basement where there were two long glass wave tanks with computers at the end of each. He showed me around the poorly lit lab and asked me how my thesis was going. I told him about the telecommunications mast with a viewing platform that I was designing, and he nodded. 'Very interesting.' I imagined him designing a far superior mast in his mind. We peered into his wave tank; it was one-third full of water, and at the far end a mechanical armature pushed water forward at slow but regular intervals. Neil was measuring the waves, their amplitude, frequency, length and volume at different points along the tank – modelling them coming to shore and devising ways to alter their pattern by putting blocks in the tank to replicate types of sea walls and groynes.

'How do you make any sense of this?' I said.

He laughed, 'I don't. The best way to look at this is as if it were music. The armature is the rhythm, the rest, as it proceeds and breaks down, is just improvisation. These machines here are fine. I need them to pass the course, but listening to the waves as they move and alter, that's the only real sense of it all, that's all I really do down here.'

I peered in at the dark water easing itself unnaturally down the tank. The waves diffracted delicately past the blocky impediments, lapped and died, then another wave washed over the receding patterns, then another.

I didn't see him again for another six months, until our graduation ceremony in mid-summer. I'd scraped an honour and he received a first class with distinction. I spotted him across the courtyard of the old university building we were conferred in. It was a bright, joyous sort of day. My parents were with me, and I assumed that the two older people with him were his. He'd had his hair cut up boy-short and when we caught each other's eye he gave me the thumbs up and I could see him chuckle to himself, then smile, and he raised his eyes skyward as if to say, 'That's it now.'

I realize, and I reckon Neil knew this all along, that a facet of our curiosity had begun falling away in those specializing years in university, like a shard of rock dislodging itself from a cliff face and slipping quietly into the water below.

Love note 5

Facharbeiter(in) – skilled worker
der Fach – the compartment
der Fachmann – the specialist

das Handwerk – craft
fingieren – to fake
künstlich – artificial
Kunst – art
der Kunstgegenstand – the object of art
der Gegenstand – the object
gegenlehnen – to lean against
das Gegenteil – opposite
gegnerisch – opposing

mühen – to struggle
die Mühe – the effort
die Mühle – the mill
der Mühlstein – the grindstone
die Mühsal – the toil
mühsam – laborious

Travelling from 'skilled worker' to 'laborious' here takes me via 'craft' to 'object of art' to the 'mill'. I end up visualizing a windmill on an agrarian plain, with its expansive timber vanes slowly beating out a type of time. I picture the cast-iron gears inside clanking, rotating and interlinking down the shaft of the mill to a room at its base that is dry and dusty and whose darkness is pierced by cinematic shafts of light illuminating men and women carrying out their work. This, from a certain angle, tells me that the windmill is feminine and that it drives the male grindstone beneath, from which the dust and bread-ready grain emerges.

In this scene a clatter echoes from above these workers' heads. This is followed by a sickening clang, then a whine, and the grindstone comes to a halt. These men and women look to each other; then, they look upward. They go outside into the sun and they see the wind vane above them continues to beat. Something has broken in the driveshaft mechanism, disconnecting the wind from the grain below.

A note on types of failure

Elastic failure is when an object, put under force, bends, but the bend is not so great as to permanently distort the material, so, when the force comes off the object, it springs back to its previous shape.

Plastic failure is when an object bends to the point of hinged distortion. The force applied exceeds the capacity of the material. Nothing can return the material to its previous state. The object is broken and it is new.

3.0 *The Acropolis*

By the last Wednesday in May, the building site had descended into bedlam. Even though we were to hand over and open the store in two days, we were still carrying out major structural works. I'd worked ten twelve-hour days in a row and was irritable, exhausted and didn't know if I had the wherewithal for the last push. Most days I felt on the edge of snapping and surging into rage.

The week before I'd overheard the project manager tell Gerald that the Irish ambassador to Germany had been invited to open the store, and a German junior minister for enterprise, with whom this ambassador was dealing, would also be in attendance.

The concrete-framed building as I had first come upon it was completely gone, covered over and coated in plastics, lights and branding. The whole place, though, still shifted in tenor between being a building site and a computer and appliances store. The top three floors gleamed all white and were filling up each day with silver shelving – aisles and aisles of it. There were high-definition TVs all over the place, fitted to columns, beams and walls, advertising products and future events in the store, and in the late evenings these adverts took on an eerie emptiness while they circulated their images to anyone working late. All of the store lights were on too, and the eye was focused towards that three-metre chunk of sales space between the floor and the ceiling. All of the subcontractors and labourers and tradesmen were gone, except for Ivan and three other Bulgarian GOs whose names I had not learned. The place instead brimmed with cleaners, floor buffers, store management, clerks and stockers. The air-conditioning system was still being calibrated and some days the heat in the place fluctuated from icy to constrictingly hot.

The place was to be stocked the following morning, a two-day blitz of products that would arrive on trucks and then be distributed as quickly as possible around the upper floors. The client was due for a walk-around the following morning too. The three sales executives would be back, this time in the company of the European director of development, a large man from Dublin called Liam, who had a reputation for being as petty as he was cruel.

During the site meeting three weeks beforehand the project manager informed us that the store designers who worked directly for the client wanted to double the size of a new display area in the middle of the ground floor. It would be called 'The Acropolis' – a hall of fame for computing innovators since the late 1930s. The customer would be encouraged onto a raised platform surrounded with stretched fabrics depicting the faces of these innovators, and while they could learn something about the history of computing, they could also try out, with an on-hand team of store experts, the merits of the latest in smartphones and personal computers. 'This area must have the appearance of not patronizing the customer,' said the project manager over his glasses to us all that day in the cabin. The display area, however, the designers insisted, had to be completely clear of structure, which meant removing a concrete column, and because this column lined up with columns directly above and below, we had to devise a steel portal frame to carry the loads from the ground floor down to the structure in the floor below. When this new demand was made, I remember my entire body slumping. I'd only just finished bringing to an end, the week before, the many problems we'd encountered boring the holes required throughout the structure for the building's re-plumbing. I'd thought my work as site engineer was done and that I was somewhat in the clear.

Ivan

On site one day I was walking up the ramp, and in the near distance I could see Ivan fitting and refitting a sign to a concrete column, over and over, until he lined up the edge of the sign perfectly with the edge of the column. The pride he took in his work and the way he handled the drill suggested to me that he was a skilled labourer or had trained in carpentry at some stage of this life. I asked him if he would make a series of small holders for the blue cylindrical rolls of paper hand towels we left at the entrances to each floor of the site. We had no materials to give him, but a day later there were five small, A-frame paper-roll holders in place, fashioned from scraps Ivan had found around the site. Between the two pastel-green triangular frames was a bar of threaded steel connecting the tops. Over the middle section of the bar was a small offcut of black plastic piping, a sleeve to separate the bar from the roll, which allowed it to rotate freely as each piece of paper towelling was ripped off. When the towelling ran out, the site cleaner would slide a new roll on, so the cleaner also got to know Ivan's triangular dispensers as things to hold rolls of paper but also as elegant structures that stood and worked.

3.1 *Alexanderplatz*

It was six in the evening on that last Wednesday in May and I was sitting blank-eyed, in the cabin, flicking through the scores of pictures I'd taken during the job. I was pondering my final task. The thoughts of working through the night overseeing the taking out and replacing of this column had left me empty. Gerald had been in five minutes before, shouting at Eugene and me for no apparent reason. All of the other engineers had been moved on to the next site a few weeks before, so it seemed Eugene and I were the only ones left for Gerald to direct his frustration towards. My and Gerald's relationship had dissolved so badly over the course of the job that we rarely spoke with civility in person anymore.

A few weeks before Gerald had run Shane from site. He'd caught him making one of his artworks, which by then had grown completely out of control.

Shane's daring and the enlargement of his interventions, I feared, was partly triggered by me. On a Saturday afternoon in late March or so, when all of the British and Irish labourers had gone home for their weekend breaks, I was walking around the site listening to its stillness and, as I snapped photos of the fluorescent tubes of light fixed to the columns in the place, I wondered if the fluorescent light in the kitchen of my parents' bungalow was on at that time too. I took three tubes off the nearby columns and lay them in a line on the ground, at right angles to two other vertical tubes nearby, completing a fragmented rectangle comprising these tubes glowing on site with the one in my parents' kitchen ceiling. I stepped over and back across this rectangular threshold of light. Then I walked off, leaving the buzzing tubes of recti-linear light on the ground. The following Monday morning Shane, as if to outdo me, had taken all of the lamps down from the entire second floor and leant them in a huge cluster in the far right-hand corner of the space, where they throbbed mightily in the dark. He'd spray-painted in an arc on the floor before them: COLLAPSED BUILDING SITE. This went like wildfire through the place, but I was annoyed because he'd finally ruptured the fabric of our game, so I stopped making my arrangements, for fear of being caught. But Shane, emboldened, continued and his interventions went from being slight, almost laughable nuisances to serious, monumental works that created time-consuming problems for everyone on site. Eventually, out of a strange perversion, people almost looked forward to what they'd arrive into in the morning and which trade would be most put out. And in this time I think Shane got caught up in the hubbub of this near-silent acclaim. One morning I walked onto the ground floor and all of the sheet-metal ducting had been crammed into the shape of a giant shining cube. Dozens of workers gathered around, gazing. Some laughed, but Gerald was livid. Another day Shane took all of the unused red sprinkler pipes lying around site and wedged them in perfectly horizontal lines between all of the columns on the first floor. It was an extraordinary sight – these red lines within lines. But Shane was beginning to look tired and I realized he was then spending entire nights on site.

Then he was gone, and no one knew anything, until a few weeks later, Eugene told me that apparently Gerald had asked the company who were installing the CCTV system to do a quiet 'trial run' over the course of a few nights and they caught Shane lugging dozens of timber pallets down to the basement where he had set about making an expansive set of steps that would run up to the rear wall of the space. According to Eugene, Shane was hauled up in front of Gerald, roared out of it, to the point of tears, then docked two months' wages and moved on to this next site in Munich.

I was sad when I learned this, but I hoped Shane would do the same again in Munich, and I hoped I would hear about it, even though, if I did, I knew that would be the end of him. I once emailed him a photo I'd taken of the COLLAPSED BUILDING SITE but he didn't respond and I didn't hear from him again. I think Gerald somehow intuited that I was involved in or at least was sympathetic to Shane's behaviour, and this merited suspicion had merely deepened our distrust.

Sunlight appeared through the window of the cabin. It broke across the office debris and cast an angle of umber onto the side wall. I looked up from the photographs on my phone and took in the colour and the tiny swirls of dust it illuminated in the space. I could hear Alexanderplatz in the distance, so I stood, and decided to go out for a stroll and have an ice cream.

Alexanderplatz was warm and busy as I ambled across. There were people sitting around the circular fountain snapping pictures. A busker sang a Coldplay tune to a small crowd of people gathered in a horseshoe around him. A few old men unfurled rugs upon which they arranged little wind-up dogs; the commuters emerging from the underground streamed around the rugs. Across the square a steady flow of customers, mostly young mothers and teenagers, were entering and leaving the cheap clothing store. A crowd of protesters outside spoke in raised voices to the police. As I rounded the fountain there was a youthful, long-limbed man with dark hair erecting some scaffolding, perspiring as he lifted the timber planks over his head and slotted them onto the upper level. He worked alone, and below him were four traffic cones with red-and-white tape strung between the tips – the plastic flapped and twisted amiably in the breeze. His work was isolated from any building and I wondered what he was constructing this platform for. A young woman with long blonde hair passed behind the scaffolding; she was heavily pregnant and wore a pink summer dress and a pair of black flip-flops that cushioned her fish-white feet as she padded past, happily spooning red-and-blue ice cream into her mouth. I continued through Alexanderplatz station, out under the tramlines and on to the other side where the base of the TV tower plunged into the earth. Dozens sat around squinting and eating, some bike and Segway tours rolled by and a yellow tower crane was being dismantled over to the left, where a large black building stood. I went to a souvenir shop, bought an ice cream and sat on a bench under some trees adjacent to a dusty beach volleyball court where a quartet of barefoot young men played with a football, two either side of the net, looping the ball over and back, without using their hands. They were skilful, muscular and glistened with sweat. A diminutive old man who looked to be of Turkish descent walked between the edge of the court and the leaf-drenched trees that fringed it. He wore a sky-blue rimless hat, and it seemed, from the delicacy of his gait, that this was his duty, to carry this hat unharmed through the world. In the café across from me, underneath the white angular building at the base of the TV tower, a woman with long straight black hair sat at a table with a friend. Both sipped from glasses of pink rosé. The trees around me were not so much swaying as swelling and I entered into their time. I peered at this pale young woman, wearing dark dressy shorts, a pair of tan leather sandals and a white cotton tank top that stretched across her lean torso as she sat back into her chair, crossing her legs. Under the table, between the confusion of shadows being cast by the chair and table legs and the nearby plants I could see the calf muscle of her supporting leg tauten into a ball then relax as she moved, or laughed, or reached forward for her drink. I looked at this muscle forming, deforming and re-forming under her skin, then she moved her leg out of the sunlight that fell across it and I peered up at the underside of the TV tower way above me, tasted my ice cream and put my finger to the top of the small spot that had been forming at the base of my neck and resolved to eat less sugar and drink more water.

I loitered around this part of Alexanderplatz for some time texting Evelyn. Two months before, she'd found a part-time job at an ancient *Konditorei* in the middle of Pankow. She wasn't keen on the work but the money would come in handy for setting up in Cologne, she said. I called in to say hello a few days after she started. She was cleaning a display area for cakes along the front of the counter, rubbing the glass down carefully. She broke into a lovely smile when she saw me. Then she nodded discreetly at me to wait outside where she joined me a few minutes later.

'So this is what Cologne has done to you,' I said, leaning against the wall, smiling.

'Ha! It's grand,' she laughed, 'but the owner's a bit, y'know, traditional, a bit straightforward.'

She showed me her uniform – a short patterned pinafore-type thing. It looked like it had been found in an old theatre. She did a twirl for me.

'I nipped off for a second,' I said, 'I just wanted to see you, but I better head back. I've a few missed calls already.'

'Would you like a quick coffee?'

I nodded goofily.

'There's a good place across the road,' she said. And we snickered like two kids.

That evening I'd to stay late on site, even though we'd arranged to meet for a drink. When I got home, Evelyn told me not to bother calling into her café again because her boss had a word with her after I'd left. There was so little free time over the following months that Evelyn and I barely ever got to hang out. She had become frustrated at me cancelling our evening plans. At night, when I'd get home she'd greet me quietly before going to bed, then, in the morning, as if all was forgiven, while I'd shower, she'd get up and make me a small bowl of sliced apple covered in yoghurt, then she'd go back to bed. After my shower I'd put on my layers of work clothing, kiss her bed-warm cheek and leave. Then, in the evening the animosity would appear again. We were limping, almost separately, to the end of our time in Berlin and I resented the distance my work had forced between us. My patience with the whole endeavour had crumbled, and some evenings, when it was very late and I was asked again by Gerald to stay behind, I'd take a hammer from the store room and walk to somewhere dark, forgotten and quiet in the building site and beat the fuck out of a wall.

*A note on why I prefer steel or timber
over reinforced concrete*

I dislike reinforced concrete as a building material. I distrust its secrets, particularly the hidden bind between the concrete and the steel reinforcement bars within. I am suspicious of the way architects employ the material to dramatically generate walls, roofs or planes of white concrete that to my mind are little more than re-presentations of an inherited fetish begun by architects who value the mere surface-sense of concrete. I prefer working with steel or timber. These materials are more explicit, more mathematically pure to me. I can understand the intent of a steel truss holding up a bridge or a walkway or the roof of an airport building or train station simply by the way it looks, by reading along its length, letting my eye skip across its main horizontal and vertical elements, then its smaller criss-crossing struts and bracings that make small language-like marks in the spaces above me, dicing the air into planes and making frames that reasonably filter my vision.

This preference of mine stems from a small timber structure I made years ago in the engineering building in university in Belfast. I was in first year and we had all been tasked with building a bridge out of balsa wood and glue, to span one metre from the edge of one lab bench to another. Then, slim, disc-shaped one-hundred-gram weights were hung from a hook attached to the bridge to see how much weight each bridge might carry. The technicians had set up a video camera to record how each structure broke so we could view the slow-motion footage later and analyse the increments of deformation, irredeemable failure, then collapse. Mine was a high, elegant arch that took almost no weight whatsoever; it warped, slipped and snapped once a quarter kilo had been hung from it. Afterwards, our lecturer, Dr Nimmo, approached me, commending me on the style of my bridge. He was from Sheffield, had a thick northern English accent, and said to me, smiling, 'There's now't like an arch.' I wasn't sure, and he could see I looked doubtful and disappointed. 'The problem with yours was that the supports were not well enough designed,' he said, 'the supports needed support, lateral fixings, to hold the bloody feet of the thing in place.' I picked my balsa-wood sculpture up off the ground. It came apart in my hands like the skeleton of a long-fallen lakebird. Then, Dr Nimmo moved away to talk with some of the other engineering students preparing for their tests.

A day later I asked the technicians if I could make a copy of the failing balsa bridges and they happily obliged. I have since digitized the VHS copy they gave me, and I spent some time looking over it before I wrote this note, which has helped me close in on exactly where my preference for steel and timber emerges from: I like objects where their pattern and structure can be seen and where what can be seen elucidates the difference between what is static and what is still.

Love note 6

die Hand – the hand
handeln – to bargain
die Handlung – the act
der Griff – handle
der Begriff – concept
der Handgriff – movement of the hand
es handelt sich – it is about
die Handpuppe – hand puppet
die Puppe – the doll
das Puppentheater – the puppet theatre

3.2 *The ground opens up*

The sun had dipped below the buildings of Alexanderplatz
by the time I got back onto site. The store sound system
pumped R&B through the place. In the middle of the floor,
sheets of sky-blue polythene had been taped down around
the column we were removing as if it were being prepared
for surgery. The column had four yellow ratchet straps
running off it, trussing it up to the four columns to the north,
south, east and west around it, so that when we severed it
from the floor and ceiling it would be held upright. Ivan and
another of the GOs were perched on ladders battering at the
top of the column sending echoes around our small enclave,
which stank of seared concrete and billowed with dust. The
last of the store cleaners stared at us as they left for the night.
The GOs downed tools and took the chance to follow them
out for a smoke. Eugene was leaning against one of the many
props arranged around the column; then he moved off and
snapped a photograph.

We inspected the exposed reinforcement in the column. This spine of steel with its congealed metal vertebrae had rusted badly over the years.

'The older guy knows what he's doing,' said Eugene as he paced around.

I could tell he was anxious.

He pointed his camera up, pulled focus and snapped again. A few minutes later Ivan and the GOs returned to the column, removed the ladders, and, to reveal the reinforcement in the bottom of the column, they took up their breakers and began hammering at its base. I looked at my phone; it was almost eight o'clock. We were a little ahead of schedule because the concrete in the column was, as Eugene and I had perversely hoped, very dusty, even chalky; you could pull little chunks off with your fingers. I envisioned the whole floor full of shoppers walking around on these slabs propped up on these chalky old columns and I imagined the form of failure this part of the building would take if a column went: a small slump, no real collapse; the surrounding structure would be called into action and the columns, slabs and beams would go into a wrong sort of tension and things would look a little skew-whiff for a while, until everything was propped out again and repaired.

'Skew-whiff' reminded me of an engineer I worked with while I was in Glasgow on my first contract, the summer after I graduated from Belfast. Colin was his name, a trim man – Scottish – in his late sixties who dressed crisply, as if he were still an army engineer, which he had been for fifteen years in Mumbai. He took retirement a few years before I joined the office but out of boredom came out of it six months later to work for no pay. He'd always straighten my tie in the morning, asking me if I was wearing it or not, then tell me he still rose at dawn each day to iron his.

He checked over all of my designs, each time asking me to draw them out on tracing paper. Then he'd place this drawing over the architect's drawing, superimposing the structure onto the building's envelope, and if my structural proposal was not sufficiently subsumed within the architecture, Colin would put the end of his clutch pencil to his lips and smile. 'Hmm there's something a little skew-whiff here, Paul.' When Colin was out of the office he'd leave his drawings strewn across his table and the company draughtsmen and I would gather around, sifting through them, particularly the ones where Colin had already decided on his layout and that had been formalized. Dotted throughout were pencil drawings – neat little sketches and quick calculations, with curves beside them, all rationalizing connections around the structure. Sometimes there'd be handsome perspective drawings beside a column or a wall showing how Colin imagined an interface working, with a circle drawn around it, or a red exclamation mark or a question mark beside it. His solutions were always so gracefully simple. He'd then give this drawing to a technician, and he or she would draught it up into the formal engineering structural proposal, and this would then be refined and redrawn and altered and refined again, until eventually a set of 'drawings for construction' were issued and with that would come a near-sigh of relief. I often wondered what happened to these earlier thinking-drawings we used to admire, were they binned, or filed away, or shredded – as I always thought, even then, that I would've liked to have kept one and perhaps framed it and put it on a wall.

My phone rang. It was Gerald, asking about progress.

'Good, a little ahead of schedule,' I replied.

'Don't say that,' he scoffed, 'damnit, we'll get this over the line somehow. We need the cert for these works tomorrow, Paul, you know that, right? Crucial. And have the place spotless in the morning.'

'I will.'

And he hung up.

Ivan was back up on the ladder. He was wearing goggles and was pushing a steel cutter into a reinforcement bar. It screamed as yellow flames and green sparks flew out over his shoulder like tiny meteorite showers, falling and dying before they reached the wrinkled polythene sheeting on the ground. The smell of burnt iron filled the air. The noise sliced the space into planes of unapproachable silence. Two of the GOs were steadying the ladder and the third held the cable of the cutter away from the sparks, shifting each time Ivan changed direction. Eugene stalked nervously about, taking photographs, trying to catch the arcs of flying sparks as if distracting himself from his own anxiety.

By midnight the column was disconnected from the slab. The props around us creaked as they took the weight. The four GOs were grimacing and pouring sweat. They looked at once tired and elated, and it occurred to me that they had been working almost non-stop since seven that morning.

Ivan jumped to the ground, dropped the breaker and mopped his brow with the shoulder of his shirt.

I nodded to him as the last of the concrete toppled from the top of the column.

'Long day?'

'Yes,' he smiled, 'no problem.'

'Good money though, no?'

He made a face as if to say 'not much' and I said, 'Couple of hundred, though, no?'

He looked at me to see if I was joking.

'How much?'

'Seventy,' and he held up his gloved hand and showed me four fingers.

'Four?'

'Yes,' he said.

'Four an hour?' I said, 'but how do you ...' and I walked away from him, as if something in the column had suddenly become of great interest. I had grown fond of Ivan and the care he took with his work and I didn't want him to register my pity so I peered up at the column until he rejoined the GOs.

Eugene put his camera down to study the ratchet straps, running his hand upon them like a farmer over a field of corn. The GO, meanwhile, on top of the ladder passed his arm over and back through the gap between the column and the slab. He was grinning at the others.

'Abracadabra!' he said.

And they laughed.

Eugene called us towards the column and pointed to where we had to lower it.

'Loosen this strap first,' he said, pointing beyond the column. 'Then you'll loosen the other two, either side, and feed them out.'

He undid the first strap. The GOs went in pairs to the columns either side, untied their straps and gingerly fed them out. But the column didn't move, the straps just drooped in two symmetrical 'u's into the spaces between. Eugene and I looked at each other. He walked around the column and pulled cavalierly on the strap running in the direction that the column would fall. I had visions of him getting crushed. I broke out into a sweat and my chest tightened horribly, like the beginnings of a wave of vertigo. Eugene stepped back and pulled again, then called me over, and the two of us pulled; again, nothing. It was as if the column stood there out of habit. Some dust and sand spilled from the tooth of concrete at the column's base. We tugged once more and felt a shunt, and Eugene bellowed to the GOs either side to grab a firm hold of their straps. He gave the column one more short, sharp tug and it began to fall. I stepped back. The blood drained from my head. The column became terrifying and my mouth widened as if to roar. Then the column shuddered to a halt as the straps either side tautened and the four GOs jumped a little, like they were stilling a giant horse, then one of them, who was holding the strap with Ivan, slipped on the polythene. He fell clumsily onto his side, and, scrambling, lost his grip, but the column was toppling again, pulling at his strap. It zipped through Ivan's hands and away, flapping and twisting dangerously in the air; and because the other two GOs were still pulling on their side, the column fell off line and slammed sickeningly into the middle of the floor. The ground shook. A boom rebounded through the gleaming store as the aggregate on the polythene jumped and a cloud of dust blossomed. Eugene put his hands to his head. I looked to the floor. It cleaved open before me. I wailed and lurched away, grabbing Eugene and hauling him to the ground, dragging him from the split I perceived in the floor, from which came a reverberating call. I yanked him by the neck of his jacket to the nearest piece of intact flooring and howled at the others to, 'Get away, get away from that hole, for the love of fuck …' I tripped and landed on my back, Eugene clambered to his feet, and as he brushed himself off he peered down at me for a few moments in terror, then bemusement. I peered across at the four GOs and realized that they had not moved, that the floor was undamaged, but worse, they had taken no notice of my warnings, and the GO who had slipped and who I reckoned had caused all of this did not look contrite enough for me, and as the terrifying reverberations in the floor died down to nothing, I rose and stomped towards him shouting, 'What the fuck were you playing at you prick? What the fuck was that?' I readied to grab him, but his face had gone from injury to the beginnings of defiance. His chin jutted out to meet me, and I'd normally cower from scorn of this kind, but my body propelled me into it. I grabbed this Bulgarian man who was well over fifty, and shoved him in the chest; and the more I saw his face withdraw to fear the more I advanced on him and the angrier I became. I thrust my face up into his and prepared to say something vicious. I felt my hand form into a ball, a tool from some other part of the world that I would use to smash this old man into the ground, when someone grabbed me from behind and threw me to the floor. It was Eugene, and he looked ferocious, but I could not hear him; he was pointing at me, then at the GO I'd attacked. Eugene's voice collected and I heard him say that he would beat the fuck out of me if I ever did something like that again. I lay there, put my head back, looked up and let my anger ebb. It was replaced with swells of shame; I let it wash over me, and tears rolled down my cheeks. I got to my feet, took my hard hat off and flung it to the floor. It bounced away. I rubbed my eyes with my sleeve and turned to everyone calling, 'Sorry,' over and over, louder and louder, 'sorry, sorry, sorry!' No one knew what to do, so Eugene approached and suggested I take a rest. I put my hand out to the GO I'd attacked and he took it. I whispered sorry, again – I even tried to hug him. He broke away and my head slumped to my chest. I peered over at Ivan, to register his disgust, but he was looking at his hand. He prised the glove off. It was reddening deeply. He dropped it to the floor; it flapped like it had been cut in two. His palm bubbled with blood. He looked up to me and mouthed ashenly, 'No problem, wash, no problem.' Eugene grabbed his hand and inspected it, 'Okay, no sign of bone, go and wash it, I'll get some bandages.'

The four GOs followed Eugene to the rear door, stopped, lit each other's cigarettes and began smoking in deep, earnest draws. They looked suspiciously at me, then they looked silently at each other as Ivan put a slim cigar to his lips and leant forward to light it off a flame. He began to puff. He held his right hand above his head, like a sort of salute, but brown blood streamed down into his armpit, so he stubbed out the cigar on the underside of his boot – it crumpled, fell and lay glowing on the ground. He stood on it and disappeared to wash. I was shook. I looked at the slab but could see no cracks or fault lines, so I left to ramble through the upper floors of the building to gather myself and reflect on how dreadfully I'd published myself to these men. A hunger pain of remorse huddled in my stomach. I walked towards the top floor, through the generic dance music pumping through the space.

The floor was bright and already fully stocked with TVs: widescreens, flatscreens, curved HD screens, all arranged in rows behind each other like waves of unnaturally clear frames of light that receded into a strange intangible distance with no perspective point, or too many perspective points for me to make sense of. Then, my haggard face flickered onto each screen. I peered up at the camera trained on me. I looked back at the array of screens again and shifted my weight to and fro. All of my shoulders and all of my heads swept across the room. I couldn't tell if this footage was a lag or a foretelling of my movements. I turned, and ran down through the store, all the way to the basement where I clambered past some barriers around the lift pit. I wanted to lie down in the lowest part of the building and hide there until I got my head straight. The pit was dark, smelt of oil and was cold. I breathed deeply and felt the air of the place chill my brow. I looked up for some time at the underside of the lift that was perched up high and I willed it to fall.

3.3 *Full moon*

As I lay in the lift pit I thought of Shane and how I would like to have spoken with him then. There is little so gentle on a building site as the minutes spent relaying a mistake you have made to a co-worker. Nearly always the worker you are talking to shares a story of his or hers from the past, where the scale and stupidity of their mistake kindly dwarfs yours and you have a laugh about it and these stories transport you, for a minute, from the present that your mistake corrupts. There was no one I could talk to so I called Evelyn instead, if only to hear a friendly voice.

I looked up into the darkness of the lift shaft as the phone rang, then:

'Hello?' she said sleepily.

'Hi,' I whispered.

'What time is it? Are you okay?'

'Fine, I think.'

'What's up?'

'I've done something here on site. I attacked one of the GOs. An old Bulgarian guy. I went for him.'

'Paul? Did you hit him?'

'No, I don't think so.'

'Why did you?'

'The ground,' I said, 'it opened up.'

'Are you okay? Paul? Did you hit him?'

'No, I don't think so.'

'Did you hit him?'

'No, just shoving, then Eugene dragged me off.'

'Jesus, Paul. Did you apologize?'

'I cried in front of them.'

'Jesus.'

'I know.'

'Where are you now?'

'Lying down.'

'Okay; are you okay?'

'I think so. I'm so tired.'

'Jesus.'

'I know.'

Then she said nothing and all I could hear was her breathing.

'I'm so sorry.'

'You're nearly done. Don't be angry.'

'I know. I love you.'

'I love you too.'

I climbed out of the pit. My heart had calmed. I trudged back up through the floors and stood beside the fallen column on the shop floor. It seemed much smaller lying there. I felt a twinge in my knee – it was mobile but brittle. I looked at the splatters of blood, then photographed the column.

The three GOs came back: this time, Wilhelm, a white-haired and portly steel fabricator was alongside them. I waved and he waved back. He'd visited site a few weeks before and exuded experience. I approached the GO I'd confronted and asked if Ivan's hand was okay. He shrugged, then joined the others, and I realized I could never talk to this man again. The other GOs carried mounds of polythene, lengths of timber and boxes of screws. Wilhelm looked at the column lying on the ground, then up to where he and his colleagues would fit the new steel frame. He nodded and left. I decided to get a coffee from a nearby *Spätkauf*.

As I walked back across Alexanderplatz the moon came out; it was almost a full moon, or in that gibbous illumination where for a moment you would swear it is full, but remain unconvinced until the next night when you see it and you realize, ah yes, now it is. It had slipped between two clouds and its glow was really lighting up the square. My heart ached at the closeness of it. I slowed and took the cigarette I'd bummed earlier in the day from behind my ear, lit it; then took a sip from my coffee. Alexanderplatz was all but empty, except for a drunk taking a wobbling piss against the side of a shipping container. The fountain had stopped gushing too and other than the faint thrum from inside our store, and the odd shout from beyond the square, the place was quiet and a little cold. I took another sip from my coffee. My cigarette dropped from my hand and as I watched it burning on the ground I thought of Ivan on the train home after this shift, exhausted. I imagined him clambering a stairs to an apartment, removing his dusty clothes, kicking off his tattered boots and walking into a dark room to lie down on a bed. Then, I pictured him breathing stertorously, his fingers falling open and the blood-line on the palm of his hand congealing, breaking, oozing and congealing again as he twitched to sleep in his bed.

My phone rang; it was Wilhelm. '*Wir haben ein Problem, Kabel, komm sofort, Paul.*'

I could make out that there was a problem with a cable, but if Wilhelm said something was an emergency and needed me *sofort*, then it was probably something urgent. I drank back my coffee in gulps, and ran back to site.

When I returned to the ground floor, Eugene and Wilhelm were looking up at a rectangular steel duct that had been redirected into a 'u' below the slab. An A-frame ladder stood between them and, to the right, Ivan and the three GOs were taping down parts of the polythene dust tent over the collapsed column. Eugene pointed to the darkness beyond the duct and said, 'Have a look, here's my torch.' I clambered up the ladder and thrust my head beyond the layer of lights and into the oily blackness where all of the services criss-crossed each other, and saw, running tight to the underside of the slab and along the line where we were going to fit this new beam, a small electrical cable, that had been painted the same grey as the slab. I rubbed my head and tried to shift it, but it was pulled flush. I shone the torch after the cable in one direction and it disappeared up through a hole in the slab to the first floor area, where the tills were, I guessed, and in the other direction, it ran into a wall covered in televisions. I pulled my phone out and rang Dara the electrical foreman. I had not spoken to him for weeks. His phone rang out. Then, he rang me back.

'What's up?' he said.

'Problem here in Berlin,' I replied.

'What?' he said.

'We need to shift a cable.'

'What colour?'

'It's painted grey.'

'Where is it?' he said.

'Ground floor, running down gridline G up to first floor tills,' I said. 'It's about five millimetres thick.'

'Electrics for the CCTV,' he replied, 'don't touch it.'

'But we need to get a beam up there tonight.'

'Fuck, Paul. I've no one in Berlin,' he said, 'I can fly one of the lads up from Munich in the morning.'

'We have to put the beam in now,' I said.

I could hear him swearing to himself.

'Right, cut the fucken thing,' he said.

'It's live, right?'

'I'm not saying this, okay? But get a chisel and a hammer, one smack, use insulated handles.'

'You sure?' I said.

'Yeah. We'll redirect it properly early next week, I'll send someone,' and he hung up.

I pictured him rolling over in his bed and falling back to sleep. I clambered down off the ladder, turned to Eugene and Wilhelm and explained in English and broken German what was needed to be done. Wilhelm strode over to the large metal toolbox his three apprentice fabricators had just dragged in and swung the lid open. Ivan and the other three GOs had begun hammering at the column underneath the sky-blue tent and every now and then the polythene would billow, flap open, and a GO would emerge with a clump of concrete and drop it with a clunk into one of the two wheelbarrows stationed outside.

Wilhelm returned, brandishing a chisel, a hammer and a set of pliers. He took Eugene's pen torch from me and put it into his mouth, climbed the ladder, put the chisel to the wire, paused, then struck the back of the chisel. He yanked the chisel away from the severed wire. He climbed off the ladder, dragged it to the other end of the run, clambered back up and struck this now dead cable again, took the pliers out, and tugged until one end of the wire swung down. Wilhelm dismounted and walked over to the dangling cable like it was a plastic snake swinging from tree and yanked at it. It slumped to the floor in front of him. Dust fell as he approached me. He looked at his watch, handed me the end of the cable and informed me that only now was the place ready.

He walked back to his three apprentices, shaking his head. Eugene and I left. I rolled the length of cable up into a loop and pushed it into a bin on the street.

As we entered the cabin Eugene took off his helmet and told me he was going home to bed.

'It's a disaster,' he said.

'I know.'

'And this has to be certified by tomorrow?!' he replied, squinting at me. He flung his helmet into the corner of the cabin.

'Nuts.'

He pulled on his jacket and then turned to me, put his hand on my shoulder, and said, 'Are you okay on your own here for the night?'

'I'm fine.'

'That was weird in there – the hole.'

'I got a fright.'

'We all get frights,' he said, and left.

I slumped on my seat and woke my laptop, looked around and out of habit I opened the architect's electronic drawing of the ground floor plan. And as if purposefully searching in a place where I knew I would receive no help, I looked at the display of the modelling space of the layout; a sort of abstract place where the drawing was put together, where the lines, curves, colours and words were generated. Each element was made up of separate layers of lines and words drawn out in different colours, then each layer was placed upon the next to make up everything that comprised the floor. One could control what was visible on the drawing by freezing or deleting these dozens and dozens of layers. I sat there and scrolled down through each layer in this drawing, turning them all on. The screen filled with an impenetrable and amorphous form: all criss-crossing lines, words, arrows and curves. I scrolled back down again deleting each layer, one by one, 'gridlines', 'dimensions', 'walls', 'windows', 'doors', 'fire doors', 'furniture', 'arch1', 'arch2', 'arch3', 'hatching', 'electrics', 'plumbing', 'ducting', 'structure', 'text1', 'text2', 'text3', 'text4' … and the drawing for a while became clearer, but I continued deleting these layers until I came to the last one. At this stage I was looking at a black, dimensionless modelling space, except for one final layer called 'stairs6', a cyan-coloured arrow pointing to nothing. I deleted that too, gaped at the screen, and clicked the package off. I looked around the cabin, then put my head back and tried to snooze. The skip at the bottom of the ramp clanged distantly – Ivan or one of the other GOs must have been depositing a chunk of that concrete column into it. I pictured the clearing of old-fashioned labour on the ground floor of the store, and wished it would disappear.

A note on statics, stiffness and stillness

A structure or any part of a structure is said to be static when it or any part of it is not accelerating. It means that all of the forces acting on the structure are cancelled out by the strength and stiffness of the material in the structure. If this balanced system is written as a static equation, the equals sign of the equation becomes a mirror, and behind the mirror is a zero.

The actual object that this mathematical model relates to is a moving, swelling and contracting thing. This object, in the hands of a good engineer, rests on the earth doing everything in its might to do nothing.

The eerie stiffness of large well-designed structures is a projection of this human version of stillness, one that is not totally consonant with the materials being called upon to make the expression of stillness. So, to cover over this disappointment, large structures, except for bridges – this is why I love bridges, they show themselves – are shrouded in garments to the point that a structure becomes little more than the painfully necessary body required to prop up these architectural shrouds. These clothes are not for the body, though; the body must contort into the shape and creases of the clothes.

My mother

There was a large structure I once worked on with Colin in Glasgow. Next door to the site was an old Protestant church, to the rear of which was a formal graveyard.

One day, early in the job, we found hundreds of unmarked graves on our site. It was an entire iron-age settlement along the eastern quarter, and within this, along the boundary wall, was the informal graveyard that belonged to the settlement. The job was delayed for months as we designed four enormous two-storey trusses to traverse the graveyard.

Six months later, on the day the first steel truss was delivered, I made a visit from our offices across town. The truss arrived in six sections, on the backs of two lorries. Each part was lifted in arcs across the sky and dropped with delicate clangs into place. These elements were then met by men on the ground, who pulled them into position. The fabricators mounted their cherry pickers, extended themselves up and fitted dozens of fist-sized nuts and bolts into the holes of the coinciding plates. They unclipped the crane chains, retracted the arms of the cherry pickers, disembarked and waited for the next fragment of truss to descend from the sky.

I waited until it was complete and the props were taken away. I wanted to see if this truss I'd designed would work. The workmen removed the props from underneath and without a second look walked back to their cabins for lunch. I got down on my hunkers, then hands and knees, and peered along the belly of the thing.

Incredible.

It was a bright and dusty day and, as I got off the ground and stalked the length of the truss, I thought of an afternoon when I was seven or so and I accompanied my mother to the local parish graveyard where her friend had been recently buried. My father's family had bought a plot in the same graveyard but much closer to the entrance, and after we tidied up my mother's friend's grave we walked to this plot and stood over it for a while. My mother looked up every now and then, to gaze across the road and hedges at the expanses of flat green fields. She was angry because I'd been fighting in school the day before. She'd convinced my younger brother and me to wear shorts to school because, even though it was still early spring, she felt the weather was warm enough and that we should let the air at our legs. We were the only ones wearing shorts in the whole school, and one boy from my class kept taunting me, so after lunch, I punched him in the stomach and he threw up, and both our sets of parents were called in. I stood beside my mother in the graveyard and counted out the free spaces to the right of my grandparents' graves; four, maybe five slots remained. I said to my mother that there were seven people left in my father's family and that there would not be enough space for them all to be buried together. My mother looked at the graves, then at me, and said, 'Hmm, yes.' She looked back and we said nothing for a while. I thought she was praying. Then she uttered, 'You are a very observant boy.'

For the first two months after Evelyn and I had left Dublin, I stayed at home with my parents. I'd been lonely about the change and was still sad at Pearl dying a few weeks before. I sat up late with my mother one night and she told me about the mongrel she had when she was young. Cosmo was his name and he once saved my grandfather from a bull. A year or two before my mother was born my grandfather, a dairy farmer, fell over one day in the middle of a field. He twisted his ankle and couldn't get up and Cosmo, who was then a young dog, barked and barked and jumped and danced the oncoming bull in rings away from my grandfather until my grandmother, many years his junior, and who was attuned to these sorts of commotions on their otherwise tranquil and expansive farm, rushed out from the kitchen to help. So Cosmo and all farm dogs of this kind since, took on an automatic hero status in my mother's eyes. But mostly, when any dog lay sleeping, my mother would look on and become quietly besotted with them. Dogs can find such a type of comfort from lying back into their own bodies, that on certain winter evenings in front of certain fires, they seem to say, yes, it is also wonderful to die.

I thought of the lake at the bottom of my grandparents' farm and the peaceful flatland skies under which all of this once happened. I imagined my mother as a young dark-haired child walking along that lake shore and the tide marks on the brown soil at the bottom fields as the gentle, fresh-water waves ran up and submerged themselves into the shore. I pictured the vertical stems of the lakeside whins shivering in the breezes and the mark that the keel of a rowing boat would make, being dragged up out of the water, across the fine lines where the thinning lake gets drawn down into the earth.

At the top of these fields was a forest that belonged to my grandmother. I used to go in there to play each time we visited her – the Hexagonal Wood it was called, on account of its shape on the land maps. It was full of ash trees, with an empty silage pit in the middle, built many years before. I thought about the summer days when the sun shone in the forest between showers and how shrill and blatant every-thing seemed in those bright wet moments, and of one day when my younger cousin who lived next door to my grand-mother and who knew this forest terrain better than me, ran way ahead of me and I followed him, but he disappeared. He was waiting ahead of me, holding a branch from an ash tree back until I walked through a clearing in the wood, calling for him, and the feeling of the world just before that branch sprang back into my face, the moment of moving, whooshing, compressed air, was so full of mystery, so sublime. I felt the blinding smack on the bridge of my nose, and I could hear him laughing from behind a tree, then run off, but I could not see him. I remembered the pain surging into the front of my face and how it had nowhere else to be directed and how this made me want to kill him, but I could not kill him because he was gone. I stood there in rage and began to scream and shake and grind my teeth and throw my fists around in front of me. Then I stood and shouted, over and over on the edge of that clearing in the shining forest, for many minutes, roaring as loudly and thoroughly as I could, bringing myself as close as I could to a fit. Then my mother appeared alongside my cousin, and when I saw him I went for him, a boar in the undergrowth, growling; but my mother, who'd seen me in these rages before, grabbed me and threw me to the ground, and, as my father had advised her, she sat on me, pressing her knees onto my elbows. I screamed and twisted and kicked and roared like some awful, croaking dervish, and she began to cry. She could not fathom where this anger came from and every now and then I'd turn my head to my cousin and tell him that I would absolutely kill him when I got free – I would say he had nightmares for weeks, months, years afterward. I continued to shout and scream, telling my mother to 'Get the fuck off me now,' and she pleaded with me to, 'Stop, stop, please, relax,' until eventually I tired myself out and calmed and stopped shouting, cursing, roaring and I slowed and began breathing normally again and I felt the wet of the forest floor seeping into my back and buttocks, and later that night when my nose and mouth had been long cleaned up and were not hurting so much anymore, my mother took me aside in the sitting room of our house and said that I would end up in prison if I did not learn to control this temper, and I hoarsely replied, 'Okay.' But she need not have worried – it got knocked out of me pretty quickly in the boys' boarding school I was sent to when I was twelve, and not with violence, but with mirth, because rage needs seriousness around it for it to grow well, something so porous as mirth makes rage peak and fall unnaturally early, then it just slips away, through and beyond, and flattens and subsumes into everything else in the world. This is how my fits of rage were greeted in that school, with mirth, until by the time I was finished there, when I was almost seventeen, so docile had I become that I was almost incapable of these fantastic rages that surged me so thrillingly close to the present, so achingly close to myself, rages that fell into the forgotten subsurface currents of my psyche; and when the time came for me to decide what to do after school, instead of looking at the things I was good at and curious about, I looked at the things I was least bad at, so I went for something useful and more or less interesting like engineering. During my first year in college in Belfast, whenever I'd open out one of the large technical drawings we were working on, showing a building, a bridge or a road or an oil rig or a crane, I always thought of the winter evenings when I was ten or so when my mother would hand me *The Irish Times* newspaper and ask me to find the editorial column in it. I'd go to the kitchen and clear half the table off trying to unfold this series of sheets of newsprint. I remembered how it slipped in my hands, and when it was opened out fully, it would be too big for me to handle and I would become frustrated, so I'd throw it down and spread it out flat, turning the pages over slowly until I found the centre section where the editorial column, the letters to the editor and the 'Irishman's' or 'Irishwoman's diaries' were laid out. Then, my mother and I would sit and read the editorial column, underlining the words I did not understand, and we would put them into a copybook, and afterwards we'd look each word up in a dictionary, and I would reread the editorial column in front of her until I got to grips with all of these strange new words and all of these strange new thoughts.

3.4 *Frames*

By half six the first of the steel frames was almost in place. I wandered up to Wilhelm who was whistling to himself, perched atop a ladder, emphatically wrenching a bolt in place. He was in his early sixties, and I'd been told that in his youth he was an Olympic shot-putter. The bulk he'd accumulated then had clearly not fallen off with the years of labouring with steel all over mainland Europe.

The three younger fabricators assisting him were at the other end; two of them on a ladder, tightening nuts, and the older one on the ground peering up at them, tersely issuing instructions. Ivan and another GO were still under the poly-thene tent breaking down the fallen column. I looked behind me. Gerald walked across the floor with his hands behind his back, gauging progress. He could see that there was going to be a delay. We said nothing to each other. He was behaving erratically and I don't think he was getting more than four hours sleep a night. He was in charge of three sites: the one in Leipzig had been delivered late, Berlin was on a knife-edge and Munich had begun poorly. Eugene once confided to me that Gerald was not a builder, he was a mere manager, he claimed: 'Gerald is a bully and an interrogator; he doesn't dream about the job.'

A thump came from the dust tent. I rushed over and peered in. It was all glowing blue. Ivan was stripped to the waist, hammering at the bottom of the column. Chalk-coloured chunks broke away and the GO I'd attacked was shunting them up the tent with his foot. Ivan was wincing. His right hand lay across one of the handles of the breaker.

'Are you okay?' I shouted.

They looked up – faces covered in dust. Ivan shut down the breaker and called, 'Yes, no problem.' He gestured at the last half metre of concrete, saying, 'Half hour, all gone.'

I stepped out of the tent as the breaker began battering again. Gerald had left. At the end of the floor the store manager was already in, talking to a young stocker. The sun poured in the front entranceway. People walked and pedalled by, and such was the clearness of the sky and the low glow of the early light, I was sure it was going be a very beautiful day. The store manager talked and gestured in a way that studiously ignored the chaos. Then he turned and walked towards the front entrance where a queue of shop-floor workers and stockers was forming.

My phone buzzed; it was Gerald, instructing me to meet the signage fitters who'd arrived to install the Acropolis in the area we'd just cleared.

These fitters were a sunny bunch from Manchester, and we chatted about their drive over as I brought them into the ground floor. They looked as if they were about to go rock climbing: knee-length trousers with straps, pockets and clinking chains.

Ivan was bare-chested and exhausted-looking while he and the other three GOs carried the fallen column's cage out of site. It bounced in their hands as they went. The sign-fitters looked on. The place looked post-apocalyptic – bright lights illuminating an empty movie set of tools and blood and wheelbarrows, and a collapsed blue tent. Wilhelm and the three younger steel fabricators still hovered above, working intensely.

The Englishmen shook their heads, scoffed at how far off schedule we were and walked back to their van. I ventured back into the shop floor. Three store workers appeared out of a lift, carrying oversized models of Batman, Superman and Spider-Man on their shoulders. They placed them down at the gaming area, strode back to the lift and disappeared. Wilhelm approached, smiling, and I noticed he had no front teeth.

'*Wir sind schon fertig. Du kannst all' die Stützen wegnehmen,*' he said, making a sweeping gesture towards the props that had circled the concrete column, indicating that they could all be taken away.

'*Alles klar,*' I said.

The shop floor was filling again with cleaners wiping down signage and mopping floors.

I photographed Wilhelm's frame from as many angles as possible. On my way back to the cabin I got a text from Gerald asking me to call up to his office.

When I got up he was on his phone while scrolling through his iPad, 'Yes, yes, yes, yes, yes, yes, yes, no,' he said, and he gestured for me to sit down.

'No,' he continued, 'and for the same reasons as Leipzig, no. Grand, good luck.' He hung up, put his phone down and frowned at me.

'How are we getting on out there?'

'Steel is up, photographed, the props are being taken down too, then the frame below in the lower ground floor. Then I'll go and collect your cert.'

'The city hall needs that today by five,' he said, 'if we miss that, we may as well go home. The place won't open, and we'll all get fucked by the client. They're here in half an hour for a walk-around. I'll be with them all day. I need you to take care of that cert, do you hear me now? And get those GOs onto the ramp too, and have it swept clear.'

'They should go home.'

'They can't,' he replied.

'They've been on for thirty hours,' I said.

'Get that fucking ramp cleared.'

Then he looked back at his iPad.

I left for the ground floor where I spoke with Ivan. The GOs had collapsed the props and were carting them away. The place was clear and Eugene was circling it, peering up at two plasterboarders cladding out the frame.

I asked him if he had seen Wilhelm.

'Under,' he said.

I realized, the moment he said 'under', that I was tired. I went back outside; it was warm and the sky was developing into a deepening range of gentle blues, and it was getting bright. I closed my eyes for what seemed only a moment and listened to the city. I have no idea how long I stood there for. Then I opened my eyes and made my way over to the neighbouring unit's door and descended into the cool quiet darkness of its basement. In the far right-hand corner Wilhelm and the three junior fabricators had arranged five halogen lamps around themselves and had lain their new columns on the ground beside them. The two most junior fabricators were perched up on ladders and fixing winches to the underside of the slab to lift the columns in place. I realized by the time I was almost upon them that I had nothing to say to them, that there was nothing to photograph and there was no point interrupting their work.

When I re-emerged back onto the street I could see Eugene sprinting into the shop floor. My heart dropped. Seeing Eugene run was remarkable because he told me once that the only reason he enjoyed the last week of these jobs was because he liked watching other men panic. I called after him. He turned; his face was pale. I followed him back onto the floor. Ivan and the others were shovelling the last shards of broken concrete into a wheelbarrow. Gerald, the three sales executives and the CEO, Liam, stood in a cluster at the far side of the space. Liam was right up in Gerald's face roaring at him and pointing at where his Acropolis was supposed to be, livid that his fitters were held up.

Eugene and I ran towards the stairwell.

'There's a burst pipe,' he said, 'an old outfall running from the hotel kitchen next door.'

In the middle of the lower floor small crowds of store workers gathered around and drifted away from a pyramidal stack of game consoles. The closer we got, the clearer the tang of rotten food became. A store manager moved people away, running a line of red-and-white tape around all of this. Eugene and I, our hands cupped over our noses and mouths, peered up at the rope of black gunk thudding down onto the stack of gleaming boxes. Eugene rang the hotel management and patiently explained what had happened, and that they needed to urgently come and fix their pipe. The smell turned my stomach, so I walked away to get some fresh air.

3.5 *An umbrella's flapping fringe*

I was unable to decide what to eat at the restaurant across Alexanderplatz. So I ate nothing. It was a small forgotten place almost directly under the TV tower. I sat on a bench outside because the *Schlagermusik* inside was far too loud. A meagre cup of black coffee was dropped out to me by a robust lady who wouldn't serve me tap water at the counter and who I'd an abrupt interaction with at the till. She smiled as she put the coffee down. I was sheltering beneath one of five white parasols shading the benches along the outside wall of the restaurant. An eight-person bike went by, one of those where they face in towards each other, all pedalling at once, as if cancelling each other out. The fringe of one of the umbrellas overhead flapped and the sun met the side of my face, so I shifted into the shade.

It was almost eleven o'clock and I felt flat. I looked into my coffee, then over the paving that led to the base of the tower. I thought of Evelyn, and her face, and how the first time I met her I thought it completely unremarkable; but the more time we spent with each other, the more my admiration for it took hold, and I don't know when this infatuation solidified, but it had, a long time ago, and it didn't altogether make sense, even then, after years of being together.

Her skin is sallow and clear, but her teeth are a little gapped and small, and she has a small mouth, and when she eats, it collapses into a thin wobbly line. Her eyes are blue, and large, and the irises have small flecks of darker blue and black in them, but I never really analyse them, I just sort of look at them. She has neat, dark eyebrows and a very small chin. Her face is almost round, like a button, and she has a long neck, too long to be graceful, or athletic, just a bit too long, and her nose loops in a gentle convex arc down from between her eyes, out to a rounded point. It is a nose that could smell around corners I often joke with her – and when I do, she puts her hand up to hide it, and says 'I know, it's terrible.' She has nice hands too, but I love her face, and I love the understated manner of her kindness. It is an inconspicuous type of kindness; it gathers around and alters situations in my life and sometimes the effects are delayed and I barely notice them, until, I realize it long after the act. It's not that she always remembers to send birthday cards, or buy gifts, or that she holds doors open for people, it is not an outward sort of kindness, it is a type of kindness that comes from her taking something from herself, a self-denial, that leaves room in the world for something else to enter into, something that she hopes will be good.

The fringe of the umbrella flapped again, so I moved farther into its shade but the reflection of the sun from a window overhead fell on the other side of my face. It was warm and constant. It reminded me of one of our first dates, when Evelyn and I took pills at a Daft Punk concert. Afterwards I bumped into some old school friends. Evelyn and I joined them and we all stayed up through the night, back in an apartment belonging to one of these old secondary-school mates. By dawn most of my friends were drifting asleep on the couches. I'd kept half a pill over and beckoned Evelyn to join me in the kitchenette. I offered her a quarter and I took the other. Half an hour later we decided to leave.

It was a Saturday morning and early. We walked into town to get some morning pints. It was achingly bright and hot. Evelyn was wearing a pale, short-sleeved summer dress and a worn-out pair of navy Converse. Her dark hair fell evenly over her shoulders. We wandered into the fruit wholesalers behind Capel Street. It was full of twisted men reversing around on forklifts in sharp whining curves, shifting pallets of fruit from one part of the building to another, and then outside. The people working there shouted and waved at each other over the din, and there was a smell of oil and smoke and fresh fruit circulating around the building and up through the florid cast-iron columns. Evelyn and I stole pieces of fruit as we ran through the place, strawberries mostly, some grapes; then we emerged, red-mouthed, out into the street again and went to an early house called The Chancery. We got two pints and sat at the bench under the front window of the pub. A haggard old man came towards us, pouring the slops from the glasses left around the bar into his own as he went. He was wearing a well-worn three-piece suit, as if many years ago he had lost an important case in the Four Courts next door and never had the heart to go home. He sat down on a stool beside us, and Evelyn rested her head on my shoulder. The sun was glowing in the window, and the river was flowing out to sea behind us, and this haggard old man who had taken a seat beside us began talking; he was mostly yellow, and I do not remember a single word he said.

The umbrella fringe flapped once more. I peered into my coffee cup and considered climbing in. I felt my phone vibrating in my pocket. I ground my teeth and decided if it was Gerald I would slam the face of the phone against the corner of the bench until the phone smashed. I pictured myself doing this, over and over, slamming the phone with my fist into the bench. It was Wilhelm; I answered it. He told me they were done and that he had enjoyed working with me, but that they had to head off. I slumped, and decided to lie back and try to snooze, but I couldn't out of fear of falling off the seat. I stood and slouched back towards site.

It was nearly midday. I went to the lower ground floor where Wilhelm and his team had been fabricating this second frame and photographed it – it was clean and precise work.

When I got back to the cabin, there was no one else there. I sat and tried to find some quiet.

Eugene came to the door. He was pale and ragged. He mouthed something about a fire having broken out on an upper floor and ran off. I fell into numbness, then turned to email the city engineer, Herr Schmidt, the last photos, and to inform him that I'd be at his office in an hour to get the cert.

Gerald came to the door. He looked tired, manic.

'I'm getting bent over a fucking barrel out there,' he said, gesturing over his shoulder.

I looked at him; I thought he was going to cry.

'I'm getting lifted out of it,' he said, 'it's all gone to fuck. We're all fucked …'

'And?' I said.

He straightened as much as his resolve would allow and I realized I'd done the wrong thing. He advanced on me and I'd say he would have knocked me out had he not still needed me.

'Herr Schmidt has the photos,' I said.

'Well go to his office and get that fucking cert,' he replied.

'Grand,' I said, and waited until he left.

3.6 *A line of windows about a metre deep*

Herr Schmidt's office was on Mohrunger Allee near the Olympia-Stadion stop in Charlottenburg, way over in old West Berlin. I ran down the quiet streets and turned onto Mohrunger Allee, a fine carriageway lined with linden trees. The treetops reached up, almost uniformly, to the middle of the second-floor windows. Berlin seems like a city that was planted first and built afterwards.

I blundered into the front foyer of the office, gasping, and asked the receptionist if I could see Herr Schmidt. She looked at me for a moment. I pulled myself together and asked again. She inquired as to where I was from, so I told her, and she consulted a wall chart behind her, sat down again, dialled a four-digit number, waited, then spoke quietly into her handset. She was in her early fifties, slim, with wavy, lightly dyed golden-blonde hair. She wore a collarless navy jumper, a pair of dark straightforward slacks, and around her neck was a piece of patterned fabric, red and white, tied in a neat bow and pushed to one side. She put the phone down, and informed me that Herr Schmidt was away on holidays until the following Wednesday.

'*Nicht so, bitte,*' I spluttered.

'*Ja, bis zum nächsten Mittwoch,*' she said, nodding her head.

'Next Wednesday?' I said, 'But ...'

I looked around at how quiet, clean and settled the office was and how civilized she was and I'd say my shoulders slumped.

She brightened. 'Is English better?'

'Yes,' I said, 'we need a certificate from Herr Schmidt today or our place won't open in time. I really hoped he would be here. It's important.'

'Yes,' she said, neutrally.

'Is there anything you can do?' I pleaded.

'This is Herr Schmidt's file,' she said, 'and he is away on holiday with his family until next Wednesday.'

'But there must be something we can do,' I begged.

'Why are you filing it so late?' She frowned. 'Have you not given yourselves enough time to build it?'

'No,' I said, 'we have not.'

'Did something go wrong?'

'Yes, lots of things,' I said. A pool of sweat gathered at the base of my back. I stank.

She peered at me, and gestured. 'Please, take a seat and I'll get you a glass of water. I can speak with my colleague Herr Haus to see what we can do.'

I sat and looked at my phone; it was almost four o'clock. I felt unwell. The phone rang; it was Gerald. I silenced it and it rang out, then it lit up and rang again, but I had nothing to say to him so I set it to airplane mode and stuck it in my pocket. I put my head back, closed my eyes and breathed deeply. I could make out the quiet drone of traffic outside.

I lifted my head and peered back across the foyer. A line of windows, about a metre deep, ran along the top of the rear wall, offering a view onto the trees in the courtyard. The tips of branches bobbed asynchronously. I looked to my phone once more, then I looked to see if anyone was coming. Then, considering the implications of what I was about to do, I got up and left.

Love note 7

die Stimmung – the mood
stimmen – to tune (an instrument)
die Stimme – the voice
Er ist im Stimmbruch – his voice is breaking
der Bruch – the break
brüchig – brittle
das Bruchstück – fragment

3.7 *Carefully placing a stone into a slot*

After leaving the engineers' office in Mohrunger Allee I took a tram back into Mitte. I made my way up and around an old church on a hill, the Zionskirche, a beautiful ornate old thing circled by shrubs and lofty trees. The sun was weaving through the branches and falling onto the arched stained-glass windows along the southern elevations of the church. I wondered how that gently fragmented light might look from inside the church and I decided I'd come back again some afternoon with Evelyn and we could sit quiescently inside, under its vaulted roof, and look at the space being made with this patchwork of broken light forming and reforming around us. As I passed the front gardens the road forked right, curving under tramlines to join Kastanienallee, and to the left it swept into a smaller street that ran up the other flank of the church, across from which stood a bar with people sitting outside underneath some poplars, drinking sparkling drinks and either reading or talking quietly with each other. I went in and bought a packet of cigarettes. The walls inside the bar were panelled out in simple rectangles of timber. Candles near the back flickered, and softly lit lamps dotted out the front. I returned outside to the warmth and bright, and took a seat beside a wavy oblong of sunlight. A waiter approached and I ordered a Weissbier. I left a message for Evelyn to come join me as soon as she was finished. She replied, saying she was on her way.

Up to my right on the other side of the road two men hunkered down, replacing a mound of square cobblestones into the footpath. They picked each stone up and weighed it, as if it were a snowball, then they would place the stone into a slot and tap-tap-tap the top of the stone with a mallet, sending strange metallic dings out into the space. They'd throw handfuls of sand into the gaps between the stones and smooth it over with their fingers, then shuffle on another inch or two.

Appendix

to bore	*bohren*
to cut	*schneiden*
to cut back	*zurückschneiden*
the height	*die Höhe*
the width	*die Weite*
the depth	*die Tiefe*
the weight	*das Gewicht*
concrete	*der Beton*
steel	*der Stahl*
timber	*das Nutzholz*
support	*die Unterstützung*
diameter	*das Durchmesser*
difference	*der Unterschied*
beam	*der Balken*
column	*die Säule*
bolt	*der Bolzen*
scaffolding	*das Schaffott (Gerüst)*
props	*die Stütze*
drawing	*die Zeichnung*
span	*die Spanne*
reinforcement	*die Verstärung* (also *Eisen*)
contract	*der Vertrag*
to estimate	*schätzen*

to retain	*behalten*
to restrain	*zurückhalten*
to need	*brauchen*
comprise	*bestehen aus*
connect	*verbinden mit*
connection	*die Verbindung*
weak	*schwach*
vulnerable	*verwundbar*
cover	*bedecken*
overgrown	*bewachsen mit*
prong	*die Zinke*
waterproof	*wasserfest*
forklift	*der Gabelstapler*
plaster	*der Verputz*
tool	*das Werkzeug*
the building	*das Gebäude*
pour	*gießen*
jointly	*gemeinsam/miteinander*
joint	*die Fuge*
to transfer	*übertragen*
ledge	*die Leiste*
the slab (concrete)	*das Platte*
the sheet (timber or steel)	*die Platte*
the slab	*die Decke*
rib	*die Rippe*
to raise	*aufziehen*
to put back	*zurücklegen*
to leave back	*zurücklassen*
twist	*die Drehung*
pencil	*der Bleistift*

ballpoint pen	*der Kugelschreiber*
stiff	*steif*
to overlap	*überlappen*
überlappen	to overlap
aufdecken	to expose
existieren	to exist
oben	above
unter	under
trocken	to dry
die Seite	side (the underside – *die Unterseite*)
brechen	to break
die Einschätzung	the assessment
ganz/völlig	full
die Einzelheit	the detail
der Teil	the part
die Trennung	separation
trennen	to separate
fest werden	to set, become hard
das Gebilde	the structure
die Kabel	the cable
die Rampe	the ramp
zu machen	fasten/shut
die Schranke	the barrier (the banisters – *die Geländer*)
die Aufgabe	the job
schweißen	to weld
belasten mit	to encumber
ziehen	to move
der Staub	the dust
das Lager	the bearing

der Lage	the position
die Ladung	the load
die Wand	the wall
die Tragwand	the load-bearing wall
der Stecker	the plug
ungefähr	approximately
der Wald	the forest
die Baustelle	the building site
wohnen	to live (reside)
die Gewohnheit	habit
künstlich	man-made (artificial)
gegen	against
warten	to wait
die Gegenwart	the present
kursieren	to circulate
das Büro	the office
die Oberfläche	the surface
die Fläche	the area
auftauchen	to emerge
begutachten	to survey
die Sitzung	the meeting
treffen	to meet
herum	around
rings herum	all around
die Methode	the method
die Gefahr	danger
glänzend	shiny
das Geschoß/Stockwerk	the storey
der Anfang	the beginning
vermischen	to blend

hören/vernehmen	to hear
nehmen	to take
gebogen	curved
die Fußplatte	the baseplate
schützen	to protect
die Größe	the size
die Abänderung	the modification
die Frage	the question
die Antwort	the answer
zweifelhaft	doubtful
das Ding	the thing
die Sache	the thing
Ich bin auf der Suche nach	I am looking for
suchen	to seek
besuchen	to visit
versuchen	to try
nutzen	to use
wahrscheinlich	probably (true – *wahr*; the truth – *die Wahrheit*)
sammeln	to gather
die Pause	mid-morning break
schwierig	difficult (heavy – *schwer*)
leicht	easy (light)
während	during
welche?	which?
wenn	if
ob	whether
so schnell wie möglich	as fast as possible
strömen	to flow
der Kran	the crane

die Leitungen/Röhrethe	pipes
die Tülle	the nozzle
der Aufzug	the lift
einführen	to insert, to introduce
die Verspätung	delay
außerhalb	outside (*draußen*)
fallen	to fall
biegen	to bend
die Farbe	paint
ganz	entire
allmählich	gradual
das Gefälle	the gradient
der Verfall/die Verzögerung	the decay
der Verlag	the publisher
die Vorderseite	the front
die Rückseite	the back
verlegen	to relocate
herausnehmen	to take out
abnehmen	to take off
wegnehmen	to take away
abnehmbar	removable
die Veränderung	the change
die Umänderung	the alteration
der Umbau	the conversion
die Umstellung	the rearrangement
das Loch	the hole
die Seekiefersplatte	the sheet of plywood
die Meinung	the opinion
die Reihenfolge	the sequence, the order
zum Beispiel	for example

die Schnitt	layer, the cut
angenommen	assumed
versichern	to assure
wieder aufbauen	to rebuild
auslaufen (ausfallen)	to leak
der Nachtrag	the supplement
schraffiert	hatched
schlucken	to swallow
die Einbautiefe	installation depth
leiten	to lead
ähnlich wie	similar to
nah	close
die Mindestgröße	minimum size
gleichzeitig	simultaneously
tauschen	to exchange
gemäß	according to
die Bewährung	the probation
einreichen	to submit
folgende	following
enthalten	to contain
zerstören	to destroy
vollständig	completely
ersetzen	to replace
die Bemerkung	the comment
die Bewegung	the movement
freigeben/entlasten	to release
eventuell	possibly
lagegerecht	correct position
maßstäblich	(true to) scale
einzutragen	to write

erfolgen	to happen
angeben	to specify
der Fall	the case
die Unterlagen	the documents
erstellen	create
Wir werden um vierzehn Uhr bei Ihnen sein	We will be with you at two o'clock
Wann beginnen Sie?	When do you start?
noch nicht	not yet
Was passiert heute?	What's going on today?
die Anlage	the installation
die Auskunft	the information

Acknowledgments

The Creators of Shopping Worlds, a film by Harun Farocki, 2001

Systems of Art (Art, History and Systems Theory), Dr Francis Halsall, Peter Lang, 2008

Germany, Neil McGregor, Penguin Books, 2016

An Engineer Imagines, Peter Rice, Ellipsis London Limited, 1994

Moby-Dick, Herman Melville, Bantam Books, 1967

'The Lady with the Little Dog', Anton Chekhov, from *The Lady with the Little Dog and Other Stories, 1896–1904* (trans. Ronald Wilks), Penguin Classics, 2002

Taschenwörterbuch Englisch, Langenscheidt, 2007

The Oxford–Duden German Minidictionary, Oxford University Press, 1999

Line Describing a Cone, a film work by Anthony McCall from his 'solid light' series of installations, 1973

Thank you to Niamh Dunphy, Feargal Ward, John Tierney, Brendan Barrington, Aoife Walsh, Achim Lengerer, Selina Guinness, Eoin McHugh, Fabian, Jessamyn Fiore, Dario Karimi and Suzy Freeman. Particular thanks to Greg Baxter.

Thank you to the Arts Council from whom, over the period of writing this book, I received two visual-artist bursaries.

Thank you to the Lilliput Press, especially Antony Farrell for always taking a look at what I was up to over the years. Finally, my thanks to Seán Farrell who edited this book.

Note on the text

The characters in this book that feature on the building site are a compound of the many people I've worked with and worked for in and outside the construction industry in Ireland, the UK and Germany. The site itself is a conflation of many different sites I visited and worked on during my previous career as a structural engineer.